A crowd had settled around Miss Turner's wagon.

Paul's heart lurched at the sight that greeted him. Miss Porter sat on the ground, Bobbin gathered in her arms, still as death.

"Is she. . . ?"

Miss Porter looked up, her face white. She shook her head. "She fainted from the pain. I think her leg is broken," she said, her voice shaking. . . .

Paul turned to her. "What happened?"

"I was speaking to the reverend and lost track of her for a few moments." She dropped her gaze and rested her chin on Bobbin's head. "I'm sorry, Mr. Spencer."

Paul stooped down next to her and placed his hand on her shoulder. "Don't blame yourself."

Miss Porter lifted her tear-filled eyes to his. "It was completely my fault. I shouldn't have allowed myself to become distracted by a gentleman. Had I performed my duty as I promised, the child would not be injured."

Jonas cleared his throat. "I'm going to have to lay her down on the ground so I can set this leg." He turned to Paul. "Can you hold on to her, or should I have one of the other men help?"

Feeling the blood drain from his face, Paul took a deep breath. "I'll hold on to her."

Nodding, Jonas reached for the child, but Miss Porter held on tighter. The woman was clearly more fragile than all other indications. "Give her to me, Grace," he said.

Without a word, she loosened her grip. Bobbin moaned, but thankfully, she remained unconscious as Paul laid her on the blanket.

Grace moved back and stood.

Paul glanced up at her as she turned her back and slowly walked toward her wagon, her shoulders slumped.

TRACEY BATEMAN lives with her husband and four children in southwest Missouri. She believes in a strong church family relationship and sings on the worship team. She feels she is living proof that all things are possible for anyone who believes, and she happily encourages anyone who will listen to dream big. Visit her website at www.traceybatemanbooks.com.

Books by Tracey Bateman

HEARTSONG PRESENTS
HP424—Darling Cassidy
HP468—Tarah's Lessons
HP524—Laney's Kiss
HP536—Emily's Place
HP555—But For Grace
HP588—Torey's Prayer
HP601—Timing is Everything
HP619—Everlasting Hope
HP631—Second Chance
HP652—A Love So Tender
HP676—Beside Still Waters

A Season for Grace

Tracey Bateman

Heartsong Presents

Dedicated to Becky Germany and the Barbour team.

A note from the Author:
I love to hear from my readers! You may correspond with me by writing:

Tracey Bateman
Author Relations
PO Box 721
Uhrichsville, OH 44683

ISBN 978-1-60260-105-5

A SEASON FOR GRACE

one

Missouri, 1867

There came a time in every young woman's life when sanity dictated she leave the home of her childhood and make her own way in the world. Granted, that time usually involved courtship, a proposal, and a wedding, but when twenty-three birthdays came and went without so much as a single solitary prospect of matrimony, one had to assume the Lord had other plans.

Now if Grace Porter could persuade her brother, Ralph, that it would be best if she and Betsy Mae Hughes didn't share a kitchen after his marriage to the mayor's daughter next month, then perhaps he would give her his blessing and let her go without making a scene. But that was highly unlikely, as men rarely understood the potential conflicts between women.

Her booted feet clicked and clacked on the boardwalk as she quickstepped her way toward the edge of town where her newly purchased wagon awaited her—fully outfitted for a journey west with wagon master Mr. Paul Spencer and twelve families bound for the so-called promised land.

She'd spoken to the handsome wagon master only two weeks ago, so she understood her brother's hesitance. From his perspective, the decision had been quite sudden. But from her own, Grace had to admit, she'd been dreaming of just such an opportunity since she'd learned of her brother's impending marriage. Ralph matched her step for step, his brooding disapproval hovering like a storm cloud about to let loose.

If Ralph had his way, she'd never get the chance to see the lush fields of Oregon and flowers that bloomed almost year round. She did love flowers, but that certainly wasn't her motivation for leaving Missouri. Marital status notwithstanding, she had no intention of playing the role of the spinster sister while another woman took over her mother's home. Betsy Mae Hughes might be the prettiest woman in town, but that alone wasn't enough to make Grace dislike her as it would most women of her vast age and unmarried state. There were so many things to annoy her about the child-bride. Sixteen years old. Mercy! If forced to share her home with that flighty, giggly girl, Grace feared her tongue might loosen all on its own. She could almost see Mama up in heaven, hiding her face in shame.

No, this was most definitely the wisest course of action. Nip bitterness and contention in the bud before it had a chance to bloom into a very ugly, foul-smelling weed. The opportunity to keep house in a prestigious hotel out west had arisen and seemed providential in nature considering her great need to remove herself from her brother's household before his marriage.

Resolve spurred her on despite the crowded street and boardwalks. The town always went a little wild any time a wagon train entered, or exited, as the case may be. Grace hated to disappoint her brother—as he had been nothing but kind to her their entire adult lives—but for once, she intended to do precisely as she pleased.

Clutching the handle of her carpetbag with purpose, she kept her chin jutted forward. "There's nothing more to be said, Brother. Now, stop fretting. It's difficult enough to leave you behind without the memory of your worried face giving me nightmares each night."

Mrs. Clyde, the town suffragette leader, approached, nodding her approval as Grace shifted her heavy bag from her right hand to her left. "Good morning, Miss Porter," she said, her double chin growing dangerously close to a triple as she inclined her head. "I hear you are making your journey west this morning."

The last thing Grace wanted to do was to stop and chat with the militant dowager. She believed in the cause, but time was of essence. Still, politeness and common decency dictated a moment of conversation. "Yes, ma'am. The wagon train will be moving out shortly. As a matter of fact that is precisely—"

"Yes, yes I am aware of that. You might be pleased to know I will be joining your little adventure."

Ralph coughed suddenly into his fist. Grace suspected the cough was more a cover-up for a whoop of delight at finally being rid of the contentious woman than a need to clear his throat.

Fighting to keep her smile to something she hoped was consistent with sincerity, Grace kept a steady gaze on the older woman's face. "Wh–why, Mrs. Clyde, this is wonderful news."

"With my Mr. Clyde climbing into heaven's arms this past year, I've decided a change of scenery is warranted. How fitting that two independent, single women should make the journey together."

Swallowing hard, Grace nodded. "How is it that you are walking in the opposite direction?"

All pleasure left Mrs. Clyde's expression, and her mouth turned down at the corners. "That fool I hired to carry my belongings forgot the satchel containing my speeches. Can you imagine?"

Ralph finally found his voice. "Seems to me if a cause is that close to your heart, you don't need them all written out."

He received a scowl for his efforts. "I have no time for man's foolishness," she huffed. "I must retrieve my satchel and return in time to move out at Mr. Spencer's orders."

"I'm surprised you'd take orders from anyone, let alone a man."

Grace couldn't contain her gasp of outrage. "Ralph!" He certainly could find his voice at the most inappropriate times.

Surprisingly, Mrs. Clyde offered a smile. "I can submit when it suits my purposes, and since I want to go west and spread my cause, I will suffer a man's orders for the greater good."

Grace couldn't help but smile at the woman's good-natured response, though secretly she would have enjoyed watching the old sentinel take her brother down a peg or two. But the books inside her own bag were beginning to weigh on her wrists, and she felt the need to move on toward the wagon train before she dropped the treasured items. She shifted again.

Ralph reached out. "Let me carry that for you."

She would have, but Mrs. Clyde gave her a look that commanded, *Don't you dare.* So, although she couldn't imagine what women's votes had to do with allowing a man to carry her bag, she shook her head.

"No, thank you."

With an approving nod, Mrs. Clyde glanced back toward the center of town. "I must hurry. Please assure Mr. Spencer that I will be along directly. I'd hate to be left behind as mine is the last wagon in line as it is."

As she moved away, Ralph reached for Grace's bag for the umpteenth time since they began their trek across town. "For mercy's sake, Grace. Give it to me. All the women except for the suffragettes are frowning at me for not being a gentleman. I feel like a cad."

But Grace shook her head and swept it away. She was taking no chances that he might hold her personal items ransom. "I'll carry it myself, thank you very much. I'm not forgetting Baby Etta."

"Baby Etta?"

"The doll Mama brought me from Boston. She looked

almost like a real live baby. You hid her from me until I promised to play the British in your war game, remember?"

A grin split his face, and he ducked his head, rubbing the back of his neck in a sheepish move. The beloved way he had about him when he was embarrassed. Grace would miss that. "Well, I wanted to be the winning army. Everyone knows who won the war for independence."

Grace rolled her eyes at the memory. After three days of pretend dying over and over again, she'd had to tattle on him to get her baby doll back. Of course Ralph had been ten and she twelve at the time, but some wounds never healed, and after all, she'd lost three precious days with that doll. "Just the same, I'll hang on to my bag, thank you very much."

"You're too stubborn for your own good, Grace." Ralph exhaled a breath that bespoke his frustration loud and clear. "I don't think Mama would approve of you traipsing off across the country on your own. Especially this time of year. Mid-October is too late. It'll be December before you come close to a stopping-off point. The snow could already be deep by then."

Fully aware of his change of tactics, Grace nevertheless couldn't help the lump that appeared in her throat. The thought of their mother and her most certain disapproval of this plan always gave her a moment of pause. To be sure, Mama had made no secret of the fact that she hoped her only daughter would marry a good, sensible man of quality breeding with a smart head for business. But that hadn't happened, and Grace had accepted her singleness as a gift from God.

When her good friend and fellow schoolmate Hattie Beddington had offered her a position as head housekeeper at the newly built Beddington Hotel in Oregon City, Grace had known it was too good to be true. She'd been beseeching the Lord for three months, ever since Ralph had announced his intention to make Betsy his wife. The fact that this wagon train was getting a late start and that several wagons had dropped out seemed even more providential. Grace couldn't be more convinced if she'd laid out a fleece. God was most certainly directing her path.

"Well, what would you have me do?" She swept her skirts aside and walked wide as they passed the saloon. "Let this opportunity slip by while I live on your generosity my whole life? Besides, two women caring for the same home never works." To say the least.

"No. You'd rather share that responsibility with twenty other women instead of my wife."

The sound of *wife* on his lips seemed foreign and only reinforced Grace's determination not to be in the kitchen when Ralph brought his bride home. She looked at him askance. "A hotel is hardly to be compared with a home." A smile tipped her lips. "Besides, at least at the hotel I shall be in charge of the rest of the women. Once you marry Betsy Mae, she will be the woman of the house, like Mama was."

"Thunderation, Sis, it's your home, too. Mama and Pa left it to the both of us." He kicked the ground with the scuffed toe of his boot. "I don't feel right taking the house and all the land. I wish I could afford to sell off more than that fifty acres next to Jenkins's land. At least then you'd have your fair share."

Her mind sailed to the vast amount she'd paid for her wagon, team of oxen, and supplies to get to Fort Laramie, sustain her during the winter, and then procure goods for the remainder of the trip after the spring thaw. Her stomach sank a little at the thought of how quickly her meager inheritance was slipping away. But it was a small price to pay for the freedom of life without Betsy Mae's twittering, flittering presence driving her mad for the rest of their lives.

Besides, she had other reasons for wanting to leave her small Missouri town. A need so desperate that she couldn't even think about it without her stomach balling into a knot of despair. Every time she passed the schoolhouse, the church, the ramshackle shack at the edge of town, she nearly broke. Even now, she felt a lump clogging her throat. She swallowed hard, forcing a reassuring smile. "The proceeds from that sale will be plenty to give me a good start. I appreciate your willingness to divide Pa's land so that I can find my own way in the world. As to the rest, I gladly give it to you—consider it a wedding gift."

The wagon train was in plain view now—the sound of oxen and cattle, the bark of dogs, and the clucking of chickens easily heard in the near distance. Townsfolk milled around the wagons, and the buzz of excitement and tearful farewells added to the confusion of such a day.

"God hasn't seen fit to find me a husband, but that doesn't mean I need to be a burden to you for the rest of my life."

"But. . ."

She shushed him with a forward palm. "I know you mean well. I also know that you would never treat me as an outsider, but I would always feel as though I were intruding upon your life with Betsy." She clutched her bag tighter and glanced toward the wagon train. "Now, you'll just have to trust me that I know my own mind. Going west feels right. I'm excited about the prospect."

"I don't like it, Grace." Ralph halted, placing a restraining hand on her arm. "I can't help but believe you're running away from something that has nothing to do with Betsy Mae."

They'd had this conversation before. More than once, in fact. With a heavy sigh, Grace faced her brother. "Ralph, I don't deny that the memories plague me. For that reason alone, this opportunity is a blessing from God. But I refuse to say I'm running away. Because I'm not." Her lip quivered, giving away more than she'd intended to reveal.

Ralph reached out and placed his palm on her shoulder, his eyes soft. "Grace. . .what happened to that little boy wasn't your fault."

A shaky breath lifted her shoulders. "I prefer not to speak of it. Now I have respected your decision to marry the woman of your choice; please respect my decision to travel west and make my own life, the way I choose to do so."

Dropping his hand, Ralph scowled. "You're a stubborn woman Grace Porter."

"I've never claimed otherwise."

"Well, at the very least I'm coming down to the wagon train with you to meet Mr. Spencer face-to-face." He gave a frown. "I've never heard of a wagon master allowing an unmarried woman to travel alone. It causes too many distractions among the men from what I understand."

Grace felt heat spread across her cheeks. "Perhaps upon making my acquaintance two weeks ago, Mr. Spencer didn't feel as though I would be a distraction." Although Grace had never pretended she believed herself to be anything more than a plain woman, she couldn't help but feel the sting of her brother's obvious implication of that fact. She gathered her dignity. "I'd prefer to say good-bye right here, if you don't mind."

Ralph hesitated. "I still don't understand why the wagon master would be leaving so late in the year."

"Brother," she said, trying to be gentle but firm. "As I've told you, Mr. Spencer's sister and her husband passed away a few months ago in a terrible accident, and he had to get things in order before he could pull out. We will be spending the winter at one of the forts—Fort Laramie, if memory serves—along the way and will be that much closer to Oregon once the spring thaw happens. Mr. Spencer assured me that I will have opportunity to telegraph you from the fort. So please, stop fretting. We may travel in inclement weather, but we'll make it, by God's grace."

A scowl settled over Ralph's face, and Grace feared their unsteady peace might erupt into another argument. But just as quickly, he nodded. "All right, but I still have my doubts about this." He opened his arms and did something he'd never done in their entire lives—he gathered her close. "I'll miss you, Sister. Keep in touch. You're the only family I have left."

The unexpected emotion brought a wave of uncertainty through Grace. Tears welled up in her eyes as she pulled back and smiled into her brother's gentle face. "I'll miss you, too, Ralph. But don't forget, you'll soon be starting another family. Just think, this time next year, you could be a father."

His chest puffed out at the thought. "Only if the Lord allows."

Grace nodded. "I'll pray He does."

An uneasy silence filled the air between them until Grace jerked her head toward the wagon train. "I suppose I should be going. Mr. Spencer asked that we all be in our places and ready to pull out by nine o'clock."

"Well, then. I'll let you get to it." His eyes filled with moisture, and he cleared his throat quickly. "And Grace, if ever you need anything. . ."

A tiny smile lifted Grace's lips. He might mean that now, but once Betsy Mae got her clutches into him, he'd be spending every dime on keeping her happy. But who could convince a man in love?

"Thank you, Brother. I'll fare quite well."

"God go with you, Sister." Ralph turned and walked away without so much as a glance back.

ঙ

Paul Spencer took one look at the twelve wagons; the oxen, horses, pack mules, giggling children, and barking dogs; and the fifty or so hopeful faces of settlers he would be responsible for as soon as he blew the horn to move out, and he felt sorely tempted to fade into the milling crowd of townsfolk and curious onlookers—disappear and forget he'd ever agreed to be leader. He couldn't understand why they'd elected him in the first place, except that at the time, he was the only single male in the group that had been west of the Mississippi.

That had been six months ago, before Caroline and Thomas had been caught in a deadly twister on their way home from town. Two days went by before their battered, broken bodies were discovered by a search party. He'd had no choice but to postpone his plans. He was the only family the children had. Now things were different. He no longer considered himself without obligation. As a matter of fact, he was chock-full of it. Four children worth of obligation. He'd never been so tired.

The children! Emitting a groan, he looked around frantically. Searching for four crazy blond and red heads of hair. If trouble were to be found, it would be from them. He pushed his hat off his forehead with a frustrated shove that almost sent it sailing. He caught it in time, wiped his forehead with the back of his hand. Maybe he should adopt the children out. He was in no position to raise Carrie's kids. They would all be ruined for sure if forced to grow up in his household.

"Something wrong, Paul?"

Turning, Paul spied Melissa Turner's dimpled smile flashing at him from her wagon. She would be traveling with her younger sister, Valerie; older brother, Jonas; and their pa. Both men would be riding horseback, leaving the girls to take turns driving the wagon. She never called him Mr. Spencer. At seventeen, she was a little younger than the kind of woman he was looking for, but that didn't keep him from being flattered when she slanted those pretty brown eyes at him.

She giggled. "What's the matter? Cat got your tongue?"

Her pleased, mocking tone pulled him from his stupor. He

cleared his throat. "Looking for Bear." His fifteen-year-old nephew came by the nickname rightfully. He towered above most men twice his age.

"I might've seen him." The seductive expression slipping through those thick black eyelashes unnerved him, particularly when combined with full pink lips that curved upward into a pretty smile. He swallowed and forced himself to break her spell. He was almost sure she was innocent of the effect she had on men, but that didn't lessen the impact.

"I'd appreciate it if you'd try to remember, Miss Turner. I need him to corral the rest of the children. We'll be pulling out soon."

She leaned forward, her elbows resting unladylike on her knees, the reins loosely held in her hands. "When are you going to start callin' me Missy like everyone else does?"

Ever-so-grateful for the modesty of her high-necked gown, he sent her an uneasy smile. "I reckon I'm not, Miss Turner. That wouldn't be proper, would it?"

"Proper, indeed." She jerked back in the seat, pushing out her lip into a pout. "I wish you would."

Relieved that she'd traded the seductress for the little girl, he sent her an indulgent grin and winked. "Sorry."

She waved her hand toward a hill a few yards from the wagon train. "Last time I saw them, they were playing over there."

He tipped his hat. "Thank you, Miss Turner."

"Anything for you, Paul."

A flash of warning went off inside of Paul. Maybe that girl wasn't as innocent as those dimples and her porcelain doll face might suggest.

He turned toward the hill. Sure enough, four, no wait, there were five bodies on the hill. Who could the other. . . ? His stomach tightened in dreaded anticipation as Bear barreled toward a small, female figure. If he wasn't mistaken, that woman would be Miss Porter. The impending impact had ominous potential for someone of such small stature.

Just before the inevitable collision, a shout of warning stuck in his throat, and he took off at a run.

two

Grace took a deep breath and looked at the wagon train. Ten yards. That's all she had to walk. One foot in front of the other, and she could put her hometown with all of its heartache behind her. Ten yards, and her new life would begin. Keeping her gaze firmly fixed on her future, she took that first step. Before her foot touched the ground, she heard a shriek, a warning, and felt a blow the size of a boulder as something crashed into her, sending her sailing into the air. The ground rose up to meet her, alarming in speed, and she landed flat on her bottom with so great an impact as to cause quite a bit of discomfort to that particular region.

Dazed, she sat trying to figure out exactly why on earth she wasn't halfway to the wagon train instead of itching in the dry grass of early autumn.

"Bear!" a child's voice squealed. "You killed her. Let's get out of here before they hang you for murder."

Bear? Grace reached up and touched the collar of her cotton gown.

"I didn't murder her, Bobbin. She'd be lying down if she was dead." A shadow hovered, and she glanced up. A hulking male figure stood over her, and she braced herself, ready to fight, until she caught his eye. A large body with a child's face. A boy of no more than sixteen or seventeen years returned her gaze, worry clouding his eyes. "You okay, ma'am?"

"Miss," she replied. "And I suppose I shall live. What happened?"

"I couldn't stop. I'm sorry."

"Couldn't stop what?"

"Moving," the boy said, although his confession sounded more like a question.

A giggle caught her attention, and she turned to find a little redheaded, gap-toothed girl staring at her. Presumably, the ill-mannered varmint who had wanted to leave her dead on the prairie before Bear was accused of murder.

"What is so funny, young lady?"

"Your hair."

More childish laughter filled the air. Grace's hand flew to her hair as she took in the sight of three more children—all boys—standing feet away, laughing pretty hard for a group of hoodlums sorely in need of discipline. "Shame on you!" she snapped, desperately trying to pin the messy half of her hair into place. "Besides," she said to the little girl in particular. "Have you seen your hair lately? Young ladies of your age should have their hair neatly plaited, not sticking out all over like the mane of a lion."

The child's mouth dropped, and the freckles on her cheeks practically popped off her skin as her face went red as a beet.

Having put the girl sufficiently in her place, Grace turned back to the older boy. "It only seems proper that you help me to my feet considering you are the one who knocked me off them in the first place."

"Yes, ma'am!" He sprang into action, rubbing his dirty hands on his trousers before reaching out. Grace slipped her hand in his and scaled the air as he yanked her so hard she nearly smacked into his thick chest. "Easy does it." The boy towered above her, his body large and, yes, bearlike.

She stepped back, forcing her breathing to slow, patting her hair in an effort to regain decorum. "I certainly see where you got your nickname, young man."

An awkward grin spread across his face. "Yes, ma'am."

Grace scowled. "What did I tell you about calling me that?"

His ears glowed red, and he ducked his chin. "Sorry, Miss."

"Hold your head up. I am not cross. It was an honest mistake. Now, as to that particular title, I am unmarried and therefore not a ma'am. You may call me Miss Porter, as that is my name." The other four children watched in silence. Grace surveyed the motley-looking group. "Tell me, are you traveling with the wagon train?"

"Yes, Miss Prater," Bear replied. He seemed to be studying her.

"Porter," she corrected. "Very well, then I suppose we shall be exposed to one another on a daily basis. I would appreciate a bit more decorum when you are in my presence."

A frown furrowed his brow; clearly he had no idea what decorum meant. She glanced over at the other children. They looked back at her with equally confused expressions. She sighed. "What do they teach children these days?" She located her bag and started to walk toward it. "In other words, please do not knock me over again."

Bear jogged ahead of her and grabbed the bag before she could retrieve it on her own. "I'll carry it for you."

"Why thank you, Bear, that's kind of you. However, it is not necessary."

He frowned again. "But Pa never let my ma carry heavy things."

Grace nodded toward her bag. "I'm sure your pa is a gentleman and you would like to follow in his chivalrous footsteps. I, however, am an independent woman, and I prefer not to rely on men. So if you please. . ." She reached out and waited.

"But. . ."

"Better do as she says, Bear," a man's voice called out.

Grace turned to find Mr. Spencer headed their way. Of its own accord, her heart did a leap. His jaw was clenched and jumpy as he scowled at the unruly, unkempt group. Heads down, hands clasped behind little backs, it was evident the children were thoroughly ashamed of themselves and most likely expecting a stern reprimand. Would he strike them? The thought of a child suffering physical violence repulsed her. Not that she didn't believe in firm discipline and at one time had believed fully that an unruly child would likely benefit from an occasional trip to the woodshed, but no longer. Some folks enjoyed striking children too much to be trusted to mete out corporal punishment. That fact had never been more real to her than last year—on her last day as a teacher.

"Are the children annoying you, Miss Porter?" Mr. Spencer's voice brought her back from the disturbing memory.

Grateful, she turned her gaze on him and offered him a smile. "Good morning, Mr. Spencer," she said. "I was only annoyed for a moment. But the children assured me they are otherwise well-behaved, and I'm inclined to believe them."

"You are, are you?" His eyebrows went up, and amusement tipped his lips and edged his voice.

Stung by the uncomfortable feeling that this man was mocking her just a bit, Grace refused to avert her gaze. Rather, she forced herself to keep steadily focused on hazel eyes that glimmered with just a hint of gold. She hadn't noticed before how appealing his eyes were. Be that as it may, she would not be mocked by anyone. Especially where children were concerned. After all, she'd been teaching for the past five years. "I am."

His gaze scanned the children. "You told the lady you were usually well-behaved?"

"Yes, sir," a small boy spoke up. "It's just like Miss Prater says."

Bear cleared his throat and frowned, and the little boy went white.

"Porter, I mean," he muttered.

Good grief, the child was about to cry. "It's all right, young man. You'll get to know my name soon enough. After all, it was an honest mistake. And truthfully, I don't know yours either. We'll work on it together." Work on it together? The last thing she wanted on this trip was to be surrounded by unruly children who obviously had no mother in sight. But that did not mean she would allow them to be beaten. She turned back to Mr. Spencer. "Are you satisfied now, sir?"

Again, the grin. How would she ever abide this man?

One by one, the children raised hope-filled eyes to her. Apparently, they had expected her to tattle to this man.

"Not quite, Miss Porter."

Mr. Spencer eyed the group sternly. "What happened?" Each of the boys averted his gaze to the ground. Mr. Spencer walked to one lanky boy and tapped him on the shoulder. "Lester?"

With a sigh, the boy, who was probably no more than nine or ten, looked up slowly. "Yes, sir?"

"What happened? Why is Miss Porter's hair mussed and grass covering her skirt?"

Grace's eyes shot wide, and she brushed at the grass she'd not noticed until Mr. Spencer had the audacity to point it out.

His eyebrow rose as he commanded the boy's gaze. "Well? And don't try to lie, I saw the whole thing."

Grace frowned and nibbled her lip. Whatever was the point of this exercise if he'd seen the accident? Did this man know nothing of raising children?

"Bear smacked right into her, Uncle Paul. But it was an accident." The gap-toothed girl gave another giggle. "I never seen a grown-up fall down the way she did."

"That's enough, Bobbin." He turned to Bear. "Don't you think you're a little old to be running with the children?"

The boy's face brightened, and Grace's heart went out to

him. He had the body of a grown man, but in his eyes shone the soul of a boy.

"I reckon so, Uncle Paul."

"Well, watch where you're going from now on. What if you'd hurt Miss Porter?"

Oh, for mercy's sake. All this over a little accident. Grace stepped forward before any confessions could be given that might earn any or all of them a licking.

"The children were playing a game, and I got caught not watching where I was going. As did Mr. Bear, here. He is no more to blame than I am. I consider the matter to be over." She gave him a pointed look. "Unless you'd like to punish me as well?"

"I don't believe that will be necessary." Mr. Spencer's brows rose, the gold flecks sparkling as his eyes danced. "We appreciate your kindness."

A warm sensation flooded Grace's chest. Gratification, she supposed was the cause. But it almost made her feel. . .giddy. And that wasn't comfortable in a woman of her vast age and circumstance. She cleared her throat and straightened her shoulders. She had no choice but to regain control before she began simpering and made an utter fool of herself. "I believe in justice, Mr. Spencer. And in the spirit of fairness, it is only right for me to admit to being equally at fault. Now if you'll excuse me, I believe you mentioned we would be moving out at nine o'clock. It's close to that time now, and I'd like to get settled into my place in line. I would hate to be the cause of our late departure."

Mr. Spencer nodded. "You're right." He turned to the children. "Get back to camp and be ready to move out within the hour."

The children whooped their excitement. They dashed off down the hill—all but one. A little boy with unevenly cut blond hair approached her timidly. He appeared the smallest of the group. His fair skin was sun-kissed, and freckles splashed his cheeks. Clearly, he had something to say.

Grace looked him in the eye, her heart nearly exploding from her chest at how much he reminded her of another child. A child whose sweet smile and wide, earnest eyes had captured her heart. "Is something on your mind, young man?"

"I'm glad you're okay. You're pretty." A cheeky grin took over his face, and he shot down the hill before she could recover her speech.

Mr. Spencer cleared his throat. "That was Elmer. He's five."

"I see." Grace had recovered her surprise enough to realize the comment for what it was. "Kindly inform the child that I am not easily manipulated."

"Manipulated? Why would you say that?"

"Isn't it obvious?"

"I'm afraid not," he said wryly.

Clearly this conversation would only end in her embarrassment. Grace wished she'd never brought it up. "It's perfectly obvious that I am not a pretty woman. Therefore, the child was either trying to manipulate me or humiliate me."

Mr. Spencer frowned, shaking his head. "I don't think so. Elmer is a good boy. Carrie used to say he was kind and gentle beyond his years, almost as though he were a real live angel living among us."

"Carrie?"

"My late sister. The children's ma." He cleared his throat. "Anyway, he wouldn't intentionally try to hurt anyone's feelings, let alone the woman who just pleaded his cause. If Elmer says he thinks you're pretty, then he means it."

"I hardly pleaded his cause." Her heart sank. Had she really thought he might argue with her? Try to convince her that he thought her beautiful? She shook her head.

His lips twitched in amusement. "Trust me. These children are in trouble twenty times a day. Any reprieve for us both is a nice change, and they'll consider you their hero."

"Hero, indeed." Still, the thought did lift her spirits.

"The children are in need of a kind face. Your decision not to insist on their punishment probably restored their faith in the kindness of adults."

Grace resisted the way her heart softened at the memory of the four children's hopeful faces. The last thing she would ever do again was become emotionally attached to another person's child.

"How 'bout if I escort you to your wagon?"

"As you wish, though it isn't necessary."

"Just the same, it would be my honor." He extended his elbow gallantly, to make his point, she supposed.

Nodding, she tucked her hand inside the warmth of his elbow. Her stomach dipped as his muscles twitched beneath her palm.

He smiled. "Now I know you wouldn't let my nephew carry your bag, but I can't take no for an answer."

Before she could refuse, Mr. Spencer leaned closer to her and pressed his palm over his heart. "Please, you'll have every lady in the wagon train thinking I'm not a gentleman if we walk into camp together with you holding your own bag. And having all the ladies mad at me certainly isn't a good way for me to start off on our journey."

Grace recognized a hint of teasing behind his sincerity. Her heart did a little flip. She despised herself for her weakness.

Rolling her eyes to show him she wasn't a bit taken in by his twinkling eyes or the beguiling cleft in his chin, she nevertheless held out her bag. "Thank you, Mr. Spencer. If any of the women in our small group are still in doubt, I shall be happy to confirm your character as a gentleman."

He grinned. "I appreciate it. I'll never find a wife to help with all those kids if I'm regarded as anything less."

Perhaps it was the heady feeling of being so close to this

handsome man, but Grace abandoned her tendency to keep her opinion to herself where matters of marriage were concerned. She smiled up at him. "Take heart, Mr. Spencer, I'm sure you'll have no trouble finding someone who would be honored to stand beside you in your noble cause."

"Noble cause?"

"Raising four children that are not your own?"

His jaw clenched. "Trust me, Miss Porter, I'm far from noble. There are days when. . ."

Grace cocked her head. "Yes?"

"Days when I don't know if I've done the right thing."

"What do you mean? Do the children have other family members to take them in?"

He shook his head. "I was approached by two separate couples after Carrie and Tom's deaths. Both would have made good homes for the children."

"I see. You considered allowing the children to be adopted."

"Yes." His face paled as though the thought sickened him.

"There's nothing to be ashamed of, Mr. Spencer. Anyone in your position might have considered allowing the children to go to a good home rather than trying to raise them alone."

"Two homes. One family, the Blakes, wanted to take Bobbin and Elmer."

The truth dawned on Grace. She nodded in understanding. "The two youngest."

He nodded. "The other couple wanted Lester. They had lost a son two years earlier who would have been around the same age as Lester."

"And Bear?"

"There's no need to adopt him out." Mr. Spencer shrugged. "He's nearly a man."

That was true enough. "Mr. Spencer," Grace said. "It was a natural response for you to consider allowing the children to be adopted. The fact is that you didn't go through with it.

They're fortunate to have you."

His brow rose, and he stopped, halting her along with him. He gazed into her eyes. "I hope you're right. They might be a bit unruly these days. I've had trouble finding the heart to discipline them much since their parents passed on."

"Is that why you want a wife? To enforce proper behavior?"

"Wife? Who said I want a wife?"

Heat flooded her cheeks. "Why I thought you did, Mr. Spencer. You said you'd never find a wife if the women in the wagon train considered you to be less than gentlemanly."

His gaze perused her face, searching her eyes. Then he winked. "You're right. I did say that. But rest assured, I was only teasing."

"I see. Thank you for carrying my bag, Mr. Spencer." She reached for the item.

He handed it over. "I hope I haven't offended you, Miss Porter."

"You haven't." She was used to men not taking her seriously. Why would this handsome wagon master be any different? "I'm very sorry for your loss. It's courageous of you to accept responsibility for your niece and nephews. I'm sure once you get better accustomed to the situation, you'll do much better. With or without a wife."

He tipped his hat. "That's kind of you to say, Miss Porter. I look forward to getting to know you better."

Flustered, she watched him walk away. He looked back. . . once, sending her heart into a tizzy. He smiled and waved.

Grace closed her eyes and fingered the lace at her collar. *Be reasonable,* she told herself. Even if this man had any intentions toward her that might result in matrimony, there were four very good reasons that she could not allow his attention.

The battered, bruised body of another child slid across her mind. Pain slammed into her stomach with a force that almost seemed physical. She wasn't suitable to teach children, let alone raise them. If not for her, little Sam Clayton would still be alive.

ॐ

Paul felt a smile in his heart when he thought of Miss Spencer. Just why she intrigued him, he couldn't quite figure. She was snooty, smarter than he, and truth be told, she wasn't all that pretty. Tiny, skinnier than the women who normally attracted him, and pale by anyone's standards. She'd probably blow away with the first stiff prairie wind they encountered if they didn't tie rocks to her ankles to keep her on the ground.

He preferred plump, well-rounded women with soft hands and rosy cheeks. And bright blue eyes. He grinned to himself. Those she had, and when she'd stared up at him and reassured him that anyone would have considered allowing the children to be adopted, he had stopped breathing for a second, maybe two.

"Something funny?"

He turned as Jonas Turner rode up beside him. "Nope. Just anxious to get moving." Jonas's hat sat high on his forehead, revealing a shock of sun-streaked, dirty blond hair.

"Then my news is bound to make you smile even prettier."

Rolling his eyes and sending his friend and right-hand man a grin, he waited for the news.

"The wagons are all lined up and ready to go. We can pull out of town anytime you give the word."

A nervous flutter played in Paul's stomach. "I reckon I should say a little something before we move out."

"I expect folks'll be waiting for you to do just that."

Nodding, Paul tried to ignore his clammy palms and nudged Delilah, his bay mare, to a trot until he reached the front of the line. He held up his arm until the fifty or so men, women, and children who were members of the twelve-wagon party grew silent. Until this moment, he hadn't truly understood just how much they would look to him for answers. The thought made him dizzy.

He cleared his throat. "Good morning, folks. Looks like it'll be a fine day to start our journey."

Applause shot up from the group. Even the townsfolk seemed to catch the excitement. They had lined up on either side of the street—some to see their friends and loved ones off; others, he figured, just enjoying something to break up the monotony of everyday life. He waited a few seconds for the excitement to die down.

"There are a few less wagons in the group now than there would have been if we'd gone ahead and pulled out in the spring. Eight of the families we started with either decided to leave with an earlier wagon train or decided not to go west at all this year. That leaves twelve wagons and about fifty of us in all. That includes women and children."

"We already know all that." Mr. Leonard Sands was going to be trouble. A big man with a big mouth. "We're wastin' daylight sittin' here when we should be movin' out."

Jonas shot Mr. Sands a look, and he backed down.

Paul moved his horse forward. "What that means, folks, is that we're heading out into dangerous territory without as many guns as we thought we'd have." He leaned forward in the saddle and allowed his gaze to sweep from the first wagon to the back. "If we are attacked by Indians or outlaws, we're not as well equipped to protect ourselves as we might otherwise have been."

Paul knew he was making a gamble by being so open, but he didn't want to take any chances that even one member of this outfit would blame him if something went wrong. Straightforward and honest, that's how his pa raised him and that's how Paul lived his own life. Tell the truth and shame the devil—that was his policy. "If anyone wants to pull out, here's your chance. I won't blame you. Remember, if we get as far out as two days and you decide to turn around, you'll be on your own. A lone wagon is an open target out here."

He continued to scrutinize each wagon and was met with determined faces. No one made a move.

"All right, then." He turned Delilah toward the west, raised his arm, and called, "Let's move out!"

Slowly, the wagons began to roll. The townsfolk waved and called out their well wishes.

From the corner of his eye, Paul spotted a figure coming down the hill, waving, the jerky movements far from friendly. He groaned. He'd forgotten about promising to wait for Mrs. Clyde. Bracing himself, he raised his arm and halted the wagons.

She breathed so heavily it was hard to believe she wasn't wearing a tight corset. But her bloomer outfit was evidence of that. Her hair had been shorn, and she wore a man's hat. Mrs. Clyde was going to be trouble, too. Maybe a different sort of trouble than Mr. Sands, but trouble all the same. Of that he had no doubt. "Trying to leave me behind, eh?"

"No, ma'am, I apologize for the oversight. I thought everyone was in place."

"Indeed?" She sent him an icy glare. "Well, perhaps you should keep your eye on your own young charges. It appears I am not the only one who is not in my place."

He turned in the direction she'd indicated as she stomped off. Appearing tiny in the dust and confusion of the animals and people, little Bobbin was sneaking alongside Melissa Turner's wagon. Paul's heart nearly stopped as he recognized the spark of a lit fuse. No one had to tell him what that meant. He'd encountered this trick more than once. The girl was about to set off fireworks by Melissa's wagon.

three

Good heavens, that child was going to get herself hurt if she didn't stop doing such foolish things. Grace had been a teacher for enough years to recognize trouble when she saw it. Bobbin (which was a ridiculous name for a little girl—or anyone else for that matter) appeared ready to set off fireworks by the wheel of that young woman's wagon. Someone had to stop her before she was killed—or before she killed someone else.

With a sigh, she set the brake and wrapped the reins around the lever. As much as she hated the idea of becoming further involved with the wagon master and his little brood, she figured the Lord had allowed her to see the child's misbehavior for a reason. He must consider her to be the proper "someone" to attend to the task of stepping in.

Slipping from her seat, she climbed down without assistance as gracefully as she could in her gown and moved forward, not wanting to startle anyone and cause a scene. The child certainly needed a firm hand, but the wagon master had enough worries without an unruly child holding up the wagon train. Grace would most certainly speak to him when the time was right, but for now, she would take it upon herself to protect the little girl.

Bobbin's hair hung wild and free and looked to be sporting mats the size of a fist. Just why the girl would elect to behave like a hoodlum was beyond Grace, but she had every intention of putting a stop to it right here and now before the child hurt herself or others.

Softly, she stepped up behind Bobbin, quite proud of her ability to do so without drawing attention to herself. "I shall take that, please."

Bobbin dropped the evidence and spun around, a scream tearing at her throat. Lightning fast, Grace snatched up the firework and threw it as hard as she could away from the wagons. It exploded in midair, just as Mr. Spencer appeared. He grabbed the little girl by her shoulders. "What do you think you're doing?"

"Nothing," Bobbin mumbled.

"Nothing?" The girl from the targeted wagon stomped toward them. "You could have gotten me killed."

Grace couldn't help but stare at the young woman. Her light blue gown clung to voluptuous curves in a manner that seemed almost vulgar despite an appropriately high collar and a skirt modestly below her ankles. Still, something about the provocative way she moved almost embarrassed Grace. Anger flashed from the girl's eyes as she flounced to a halt in front of Mr. Spencer, and Grace had the urge to draw the child behind her skirts and protect her.

Bobbin, however, seemed able to hold her own. She kept her mouth shut, but the sheer look of hatred she flashed the young woman was enough to peel the paint off a barn door.

"What do you have to say for yourself, young lady?" Mr. Spencer demanded.

The little girl shrugged, no hint of repentance in her demeanor or expression. As a matter of fact, not only was she not repentant, she folded her arms across her chest in belligerence and planted her feet hip distance apart as though daring anyone to punish her.

Mr. Spencer frowned, crossed his own arms over his chest and matched her glare for glare. "Well?"

"She was trying to kill me," the girl from the wagon said. She slipped her hand through his arm, wrapping her fingers around his bicep. "Paul, you will punish her, won't you?"

He covered her hand and looked down at her in sympathy. "I'm sorry, Miss Turner. I'm sure Bobbin is sorry, too."

An unfamiliar pang slammed Grace full in the gut. Jealousy? Certainly not! She fought a contemptuous stare at Miss Turner, almost sorry she'd interfered with the attempted sabotage. Well, no. That wasn't nice. Even if Miss Turner was an annoying temptress, she didn't deserve harm because of it.

"I'm sure Bobbin wants to apologize to you, Miss Turner." Paul glanced toward the wagons, where heads craned to see what was happening. None too patiently, either.

"Apologize, my foot." Miss Turner stomped like a petulant child sorely in need of a paddling herself. Her chest heaved with her indignation. "I demand that you deal with that child immediately."

"Folks are waiting—"

"Mr. Spencer," Grace said, standing behind Bobbin and planting her hands on the little girl's shoulders. "Perhaps we should continue with our plans to begin our journey for now, and you can deal with Bobbin when we stop for our noon meal."

He hesitated.

"The child may share my wagon and keep me company." Not until the words left her lips did Grace intend to speak them. Now that the gesture had been made, she prayed Mr. Spencer would refuse the offer. She of all people wasn't fit to supervise children. She no longer possessed the judgment for the task.

Miss Turner stomped her foot again and huffed, clearly expressing her disapproval of the suggestion. Ignoring her, Grace kept her steady gaze focused on Mr. Spencer.

He peered closer at Grace. "Are you sure you wouldn't mind? I don't want to impose. Believe me, Bobbin can be a handful."

She tried not to let her hesitation show, but from the wagon master's frown, she knew he'd noticed.

"It's all right," he said. "I'll let her ride on my horse with me."

Suspicion tinged Grace's mind as she weighed his words, but only for a second. Mr. Spencer's eyes shone with too much earnest appeal for him to be making an attempt at manipulation. "Surely you will be too busy with your own duties as wagon master to be encumbered with the responsibility of a child. Particularly on the first day of our journey."

He shrugged. "I'm sure we'll make out just fine."

Drawing a full breath, Grace slipped her arm around Bobbin's shoulders and drew the girl close against her side. "My solution will keep the child out of trouble and force her to remain supervised the rest of the day while you attend your duties."

Bobbin turned her head and looked up, her eyes wide with a most unflattering flicker of pure horror, the emotion which Grace had to admit served the child right. She had no business enjoying herself until she was sufficiently punished for her shenanigans.

"There is no need to delay the child's punishment," Miss Turner huffed. "After all, she might have killed me."

"Miss Turner," Paul began, "I assure you Bobbin will be dealt with. But for now, fifty people have waited long enough to begin their journey. Miss Porter's solution seems sensible and much appreciated, in light of our need to move out as soon as possible." His expression remained grim, stern, as he directed his attention to his niece. "You stay with Miss Porter today. And I'd advise you to be on your best behavior. I'll deal with you later."

The little girl kicked at the ground with scuffed boots. "Aw, Uncle Paul. Can't I go back to our wagon and ride with Bear?"

"No. If he'd have been watching you in the first place, you wouldn't be causing trouble."

"Don't blame Bear, Uncle Paul. I snuck off when he wasn't looking."

Once more, Miss Turner stomped her delicate boot on the ground. "Does this mean you're letting her off scot-free?"

"Come, Bobbin," Grace said, directing the little girl toward her wagon. "We can let these two settle their own differences."

Somehow, Mr. Spencer disentangled from Miss Turner's clutches and fell into step alongside Grace just as they reached her wagon. "Thank you, Miss Porter."

"No thanks are necessary." She dropped her tone. "But I hope it will not happen again."

"I'll see that it doesn't." He sent her a wink that brought a rush of heat to her cheeks. She knew she sounded shrewish. But if he only knew her reasons, perhaps he wouldn't judge her too harshly.

"Paul!" Miss Turner's insistent voice spared her the necessity of forming a response as the young woman stalked up behind them and grabbed onto Paul's sleeve. "Are you going to help me into my wagon? It's the least you can do since your girl almost killed me."

Paul gave only the merest hint of hesitation, then turned to her. "It will be my pleasure, Miss Turner. As soon as Bobbin apologizes to you."

Grace pursed her lips. She supposed he was right. But Miss Turner certainly appeared to deserve whatever orneriness the children might devise. Of course, she'd never admit such a thing. But it must have been plastered on her face because Mr. Spencer winked at her. Winked! "Don't you agree, Miss Porter? The child showed bad manners, and Miss Turner might have been hurt if you hadn't thwarted her efforts at sabotage."

Before she could answer, Miss Turner's eyebrows rose in haughty indignation. "Well?" She planted her hands on her hips and stared a hole into Bobbin. . .waiting.

The little girl tensed, and for a second, Grace thought she might refuse. Then a sneer curled her pink little lips, and she glared at the young woman. "Sor—ry."

"All right, let's go," Grace said.

"Go?" Miss Turner sniffed. "Surely you don't believe she meant it."

Tired of the spoiled young woman's outbursts, Grace spoke up before Mr. Spencer decided to force the child to sound more sincere. "Miss Turner," she said, regarding the girl with her most stern, schoolteacher stare, "the child has apologized as she was told to do. *Paul*, as you call him, did not tell the child to mean it. Only that she must say it."

Miss Turner's jaw dropped, and chest heaving, she seemed unable to form a reply.

Grace smiled. "I see you understand my point. Good day, Miss Turner. Try not to kick up too much dust today, please, as we shall be directly behind you."

Miss Turner's face grew red with fury. Her mouth opened and closed a couple of times, but she couldn't seem to form a retort. Rather, she whipped around and stomped toward her wagon.

Grace watched her, a sense of satisfaction shooting through. She nudged Bobbin's shoulder. "Come along, Bobbin."

"Yes, ma'am."

"Miss."

"Yes, Miss Porter," Bobbin replied meekly.

Without another word, they turned back toward Grace's wagon. Bobbin patted the ox as she passed by the enormous beast and then scrambled into the wagon seat without waiting for Grace's help.

Grace moved to the other side and reached up. But before she could climb into her seat, a hand reached out. She turned to find Mr. Spencer mere inches from her. "I'll help."

"It isn't necessary." Why on earth was she suddenly breathless?

"Indulge me. It's the least I can do for your assistance."

Slipping her hand into his, she nodded. "Very well."

"And thank you for helping me with Bobbin and for putting Miss Turner in her place."

"Why I did no such thing." She plopped into the seat.

He chuckled. "Yes, you did. She might not recover from not getting her way." He turned to Bobbin, and his tone dropped to a stern warning. "You'd best behave."

"Yes, sir."

Grace unwrapped the reins from the brake and readied herself to move out when the call came. She turned to Bobbin. "Reach behind the seat and grab my bag, please."

The child stood and used both hands, pulling the red carpetbag from its spot. "This?"

"Yes. Now, please reach inside and pull out the brush."

Suspicion clouded the little girl's eyes, and Grace came near to smiling. But she remained firm, knowing that this child was as much in sore need of discipline as she was of grooming. "Why do you need your brush when you're driving the oxen?"

"I think you can judge my reasons for yourself."

The child snatched the brush from the bag with a huff. She pushed it toward Grace. Grace shook her head. "You are big enough to brush your own hair."

Bobbin's eyes grew wide. "I am?"

"Of course. And you will do so as long as you're riding with me. When we stop for lunch, I will fasten it into braids."

"With ribbons?"

Her heart went out to the little girl. Maybe she'd misjudged her actions as tomboyish ways when she merely needed a woman's hand to help her. The child obviously wanted to wear pretty things. "Possibly. If you get all the knots out by then." She cut Bobbin a glance and a challenge. "But that feat is highly unlikely."

In a flash, the little girl took up the challenge and went to work, wincing when the bristles pulled against the tangles.

Grace turned away so the child couldn't see the smile on her lips. As she did so, her eyes caught Mr. Spencer's gaze. He smiled as though returning hers. The moment felt intimate, as though they shared a secret.

Lifting his arm, he turned his horse and called, "Move out."

four

Paul held tightly to Delilah's reins as the mare tensed with the excitement of new movement. Paul knew how she felt. He'd love nothing more than to allow her to open up and let the wind splash against his face for as long as she wanted to run west. But he felt the weight of responsibility as slowly the wagons began to roll forward. Swaying over the road, pots and pans clattered where they hung off the wagon walls. Chickens squawked in their makeshift pens inside wagons, and cows—the five accompanying them west—mooed against their tethers.

His mind returned to Miss Porter and the way she handled Bobbin. She continued to surprise him. Beneath her persnickety behavior beat the heart of a gentle woman with a good nature. The children had discovered her sympathetic side immediately and played into it fully. He couldn't help but smile at her when he noticed Bobbin pulling a brush through her matted hair. He'd tried, heaven knew he had, to get that girl to brush her hair. Bobbin's insistence that the pain was more than she could bear had softened him, and he hadn't found the heart to force the misery upon her. Apparently, Miss Porter was having none of Bobbin's excuses.

Pulled from his thoughts, he turned to Jonas Turner.

"What did you do to upset my little sister?" Jonas asked, a smirk twisting his lips.

A groan escaped Paul's lips. He'd forgotten all about Melissa. "My niece nearly set off fireworks by her wagon wheel, I'm afraid."

"That explains why she's mad at the little girl." He gave

a short laugh. "I almost wish she'd have succeeded. I might have enjoyed seeing Melissa land on her behind."

"She might have been hurt."

That thought sobered the fun-loving Jonas. "So why is she mad at you? She refused to say."

Wiping sweat from his brow with the back of his hand, Paul shook his head. "I haven't punished Bobbin yet. Your sister felt like I should have been a little more heavy-handed on the spot." Not to mention the fact that he hadn't followed her to her wagon and assisted her into the seat. But there was no point in bringing that up, the reasons he'd given seemed to satisfy Jonas. As a matter of fact, Jonas seemed to be getting a lot of entertainment from the entire situation.

Jonas whooped. "Melissa never got a whipping herself. Not that she didn't deserve plenty of them. And she's suggesting punishment for your girl?"

Uncomfortable discussing a private situation, Paul cleared his throat and changed the subject. "Everyone rolling along okay?"

"You mean in the last ten minutes since we started?" He grinned.

"Yeah." Paul returned his grin, a bit sheepishly.

"So far so good." Jonas pulled his horse's reins. "I'll rove to the back of the line and check again."

Paul watched him go. Jonas was going to have to pace himself or he'd wear out his horse before they'd gone three miles.

He couldn't believe they were finally going west. The sight of the pioneers looking forward to a new life caused a conflict of emotions inside of him. On one hand, his excitement mirrored theirs. But mostly, he felt the loss of Caroline and Thomas more than ever today. His sister and brother-in-law had planned to make the westward trek, dreamed of making a new life for their four children. Determination rose high inside Paul's chest. If his sister couldn't make the dream live for her children, he would do it for her.

He looked around for at least the tenth time in the last few minutes to check and make sure all the children were accounted for. Bear was stuck driving their wagon, much to the boy's dismay. Paul hated to force the confinement on the lad, but there was no one else to do it. Who else among the children was strong enough to keep the oxen pulling the right direction? Lester? Paul smiled at the ridiculous thought.

By noon, the wagon train had traveled seven miles. Good time spurred on, Paul knew, by the enthusiasm in everyone's gut. Twelve-year-old Lester smiled up from the fire as he approached. "I made some coffee for you, Uncle Paul."

Lester endured more than his fair share of teasing for enjoying the role of cook in the family, but Paul had to admit that he was grateful. "Thank you, son," he said, accepting a tin cup of the steaming brew. "I'm obliged."

The boy beamed under the praise. "Bacon will be done soon, and I wrapped up the leftover biscuits from breakfast."

"That's fine, Lester."

"Sure," Bear teased. "That's fine, *Ma*."

Lester glowed red. Anger flashed in his eyes. Typically, Paul tried not to interfere in these sorts of quarrels. But when Lester's hands squeezed into fists, he knew he'd better step in. "Listen, you hoodlums. You'd best be glad your brother can cook. Otherwise, we'd all starve before we reach Oregon."

"When's Bobbin coming back?" Elmer asked. "I miss her." The closest in age, the two were inseparable on most occasions.

"She's riding with Miss Porter to keep herself out of trouble." Paul squinted over the rim of his cup. He swallowed. "Who put her up to the fireworks, anyway?"

Bear and Lester averted their eyes from his gaze. Only Elmer kept eye contact, a sign of the little boy's innocence. "That's what I thought. Why do you goad her into getting herself into trouble? And what do you have against Miss Turner?"

"She's got her cap set for you, Uncle Paul."

"What do you know about such things?"

Lester wrinkled his freckled nose. Then he batted his eyes and clasped his hands in front of his chest. "Oh, Paul, you're so strong." Bear and Elmer howled with laughter.

"I declare," Bear said, picking up where Lester left off and doing a lady's voice that wasn't too convincing in the boy's cracking baritone. "You're so handsome." He made a vigilant effort though, patterning Lester's pose, clasping his enormous hands and batting his eyes. The attempt at a high-pitched voice even brought a smile to Paul's lips. "That's enough," he said, firmly. "Miss Turner is a lovely girl and is much too young and pretty to give a grizzled old rancher like me a second thought."

"Why, Paul, that's so sweet." For a second, Paul tried to figure out which of the boys was mimicking Miss Turner so well; then, with an inward groan, he realized Melissa was indeed standing at the edge of camp and had heard his words. He stood as she approached and removed his hat. Her long lashes did bat a little as she looked up at him with a coquettish smile. "Did you mean it?"

A smile tipped his lips as she fished for a compliment. "I never say anything I don't mean."

"And here I was determined that I would never forgive you for your behavior earlier."

Irritation slithered through his chest at the reminder of her harsh attitude toward Bobbin. Not that the little girl didn't deserve punishment. But Miss Turner's attitude was only slightly more grown-up than the little girl herself. Still, he had to remember the way his ma had raised him. He had no choice but to behave as a gentleman. "I appreciate your gracious forgiveness, Miss Turner."

"What do you want, anyway?" Lester said, the boy's face twisted in disdain.

"Les, show your manners," Bear said, backhanding the boy in the back of the head.

"Ow!" Lester huffed and turned his frown back to Miss Turner. "What do you want anyway, *miss*?"

Miss Turner's lips pursed in disapproval, and Paul stiffened, anticipating a scene similar to the one that morning with Bobbin. Thankfully, she seemed more interested in delivering whatever message she had on her mind. "Paul, I thought you might enjoy having dinner with our family tonight."

"I thought you weren't gonna forgive him 'til you heard him say you was pretty," Lester reminded her, most ill-manneredly.

Her eyes glittered with irritation, but she reined in her emotions and smiled at Paul. "I suppose I couldn't have stayed mad at you no matter what. Please say you'll come."

Her eyes drew him in, and Paul couldn't help but respond to those full lips, parted and turned upward. He cleared his throat.

"Please say yes," she said with a pretty pout.

"All right. We'll be there."

Her eyes grew wide. "We?" She glanced down. "Oh. There are the children to consider as well, aren't there?"

"Yes."

"She don't want us," Lester spat. "I'd rather eat a rattlesnake than eat with her anyhow."

"Yeah," Elmer shoved in before Paul could shush them. "I bet Lester cooks a lot better than her."

"Listen," Miss Turner said. "Of course you're all welcome to join us. Jonas brought down four rabbits this morning and I'm making a nice rabbit stew."

"I like 'em better roasted."

"That's enough," Paul said, finally stepping in. He turned to Miss Turner. "Thank you for your kind invitation. We'll be there."

Dimples flashing, she smiled, sashayed closer to him, and touched his arm. "I'm so glad our little misunderstanding earlier today is over. I'll look forward to it."

The boys scowled as they watched her go. "I don't like it, Uncle Paul," Lester said, shaking his head.

"What don't you like?"

"Eating over there. It don't look good. She wants you to court her, and it don't matter to her if you're nothing more than a grizzled old rancher."

"He's right, Uncle Paul," Elmer said. "And I don't like it, either."

Paul grinned down at the little boy and slipped his arm around his shoulders, drawing him close. "What's a five-year-old boy know about women?"

As Paul knew he would, Elmer grinned, blushed, and giggled. "Nothing."

"Then mind your own business."

"I like Miss Porter best," Lester said.

"Me, too," Bear spoke up. The gentle young man rarely voiced his opinion. When he did, Paul knew he meant what he said.

Paul stood. The fire hissed as he tossed the remains of his cup into it. "Eat your lunch and clean up," he said, "we'll be moving out in thirty minutes."

"Don't you want to eat?" Lester said.

"Aw," Elmer piped up. "He's probably goin' to eat with that Miss Turner."

"Nope," Paul said. "I'm going to go check on Bobbin."

"Wait," Lester said. He handed Paul a plate with two biscuits and some bacon. "Take this with you. You didn't eat."

Paul's heart shifted as he took the plate from the child's hand. Somehow, instead of him taking care of his niece and nephews, they had taken on the responsibility for his future.

The thought weighed heavily on his mind as he headed

toward Miss Porter's wagon. They needed a mother. Plain and simple. His thoughts turned to Miss Turner. Jonas's sister was beautiful and could make any man's blood warm, but as a mother to the children? He couldn't even imagine a happy home with the six of them clashing all the time. He pushed aside all thoughts of the tempting young woman as he approached Miss Porter's campfire.

His eyebrows rose at the sight of Bobbin, seated on a pickle barrel, legs swinging, chatting amiably with Miss Porter. She hopped up at the sight of him and ran into his arms. "Look at my ribbons. Miss Porter gave them to me."

At the end of two long braids were indeed two pink bows. "Very pretty, Bobbin. Did you thank Miss Porter?"

"Of course she did, Mr. Spencer." Miss Porter stood over a fire. She nodded toward the plate in his hand. "I see you brought your lunch with you, but may I offer you a cup of coffee?"

"Much obliged."

"You may have a seat over there on the barrel."

"Thank you."

He took a cup from her. "I see things are going well with Bobbin."

"Yes. The child is agreeable enough. She enjoys words. We had something of a spelling bee while we rode along."

"You don't say?" Eyebrows up, he turned to Bobbin, who shrugged.

"Don't tell the boys, okay?"

"I give you my word." His lips twitched. It certainly would never do if anyone thought she might enjoy learning.

Though the temperature was mild, the sun overhead beat down, producing beads of perspiration on Miss Porter's forehead. She wiped them away with the back of her arm as she handed Bobbin a plate of warmed stew and a slice of bread. "If you eat all of that, you may have a slice of apple pie."

Bobbin's eyes grew wide. "Yes, Miss Porter." Her eyes twinkled as she looked at Paul. "Won't the boys be jealous?"

"I suppose they will," Paul said.

"Well, that certainly isn't the idea." A smile touched the corners of Miss Porter's lips, but Paul noted she didn't allow Bobbin to see her amusement. "Perhaps you should take a pie to your wagon tonight. They might each like a slice after their evening meal."

"Can we, Uncle Paul?"

Paul's mouth watered at the thought of pie. But he shook his head. "We can't take Miss Porter's pie. There's no telling when she'll have more."

Miss Porter's eyebrows rose as though gauging his sincerity. "I can't possibly eat three pies alone before they go bad."

"Three pies?"

"My brother's bride-to-be was so thrilled to get rid of me she went a little overboard on parting gifts." She gave a little laugh. "I am also stocked with several loaves of bread that will likely turn moldy long before I'm able to eat them all and an entire basket of apples from her parents' orchard. She also sent enough beef stew for a small army."

"See, Uncle Paul?" Bobbin's eyes were widely innocent as she pressed for the treats. "Mama always said waste not want not."

"If it will make you feel better, Mr. Spencer, you may take a share of the bread and stew as well. I'd actually be grateful. Otherwise I'll be forced to toss most of the food."

Bobbin turned from Miss Porter to Paul. "Please, Uncle Paul?"

Paul cringed inside. He hesitated. "Actually, we've already been invited to supper."

Bobbin's brow creased. "By who?"

"Whom," Miss Porter corrected. "It's quite all right. I'm sure the Adams' dog will appreciate the leftovers. He seems a bit scrawny anyway."

Relief flooded Paul that he wouldn't be obliged to reveal who had extended the invitation. Or was that *whom*? He sipped his coffee and caught Miss Porter's eye. Heat crept to his cheeks at her knowing look. She turned away to cut into the pie.

Bobbin scowled, not as inclined to let it go as Miss Porter. "But who invited us to supper?"

Miss Porter handed Bobbin her pie. "Don't be impolite, Bobbin. Please eat your pie." She turned her attention to Paul. "I assume it's almost time to resume our journey."

Paul nodded, chewing a bite of bacon. He tossed the rest of his meal into the fire and stood. He fixed his gaze on Bobbin. "Come to our wagon as soon as we call a stop for the evening." He looked up at Miss Porter. "We won't travel too far tonight with it being our first night on the trail."

Relief crossed her features. "Easing us into the situation is probably for the best."

Shifting from one foot to the next, Paul hesitated.

"Was there something else, Mr. Spencer?"

Why did he feel the urge to apologize? Paul hadn't been this addled since he fell off Delilah before she was fully broken. Irritated, he scowled. What did he have to be sorry for anyway? He certainly wasn't committing a crime by accepting a dinner invitation from a lovely young woman who, as the children feared, seemed to have her cap set for him. Miss Porter barely acknowledged him and certainly not in that way.

"Mr. Spencer?" Her waiting tone irked him.

"Never mind."

He stomped to his tethered horse, mounted, and made his way down the line of wagons—steering clear of Miss Porter's. She knew to start preparations for departure anyway.

Within twenty minutes, folks had doused their fires,

packed up, and were ready to resume the second half of the first day westward. With two women on his mind, Paul figured he'd be insane by Christmas.

five

Grace tried not to be consumed with the thought that Mr. Spencer and the children were going to another woman's fire for dinner. Really, why should she care if the man wanted to court an impossible young woman who was completely unsuitable to become a mother to four children? Melissa Turner was barely a day older than Bear as it was. What on earth could Mr. Spencer possibly be thinking? She certainly wasn't a mother herself, but Grace couldn't help but wonder what the children's mother would think about Melissa Turner taking over her children. And she was almost positive that no sister would approve of Melissa as a choice for her brother any more than Grace approved of Betsy Mae for Ralph.

At the very thought, Grace's face bloomed. Surely her face must already be red enough from the sun's rays to cover her embarrassment.

Bobbin skipped alongside the wagon. Grace hadn't had the heart to deny her the little pleasure of stretching her legs a bit, despite the fact the child was being punished for her poor behavior earlier that day. She watched the child under hooded lids. To Grace's surprise, Bobbin had turned out to be a more than welcome companion. In less than a day, she had given over her resolve not to get involved with children again. But she couldn't very well ignore a child entrusted to her care. Besides, it was only for today. Mr. Spencer would make other arrangements by tomorrow as he had promised.

For now, as the little girl skipped and played, providing her own enjoyment, she kept Grace entertained against the monotony of one wagon roll after another without much change in the scenery. Prairie grass, brown and withered, sprouted up to Bobbin's knees. Her little hands grazed the tops of the waving grass as she played.

From the corner of her eye, Grace noted a rider on horseback and turned, her heart jumping as she expected to find Mr. Spencer there. Instead, a slim, fortyish man, wearing a black suit of clothing—parson's clothes, with a hat to match—looked down at her. His face was pleasant enough, if a bit shaggy along the jawline, no doubt in an attempt to grow a beard. He tipped his hat. "How-do, ma'am."

"Miss," she corrected. "And I do quite well, thank you."

He looked flustered but covered it well enough. "I thought I'd introduce myself," he said. "My name is Ellis. *Reverend* Ellis."

Grace smiled. "My name is Grace Porter. *Miss* Porter." She reached out her hand. "Pleased to meet you, Reverend."

A smile curved his lips and brightened his eyes, which appeared to be blue, but with the sun bright behind him, she couldn't be sure. "Delighted to meet you as well, Miss Porter."

"Is your family traveling with you, Reverend?"

His face clouded a bit. "I'm afraid I am bereft of family, Miss Porter. My wife has been gone now for the past ten years."

"I'm sorry," Grace murmured.

"That's most kind of you." He smiled kindly. "So far, God has not seen fit to bless me with a wife with whom I might grow old, so like Saint Paul, I have remained single."

Embarrassment flooded her at his frank manner. "I suppose that's the most sensible course of action."

"Am I to assume you have never married, Miss Porter?"

Irritation flooded her. How could a man of God be so forward and so ill-mannered as to bring attention to the obvious fact that no man had wanted her? She lifted her chin. "I suppose you may assume whatever you wish, Reverend Ellis."

He leaned closer and frowned. "I see I've offended you with my foolish blubbering. Please forgive me, Miss Porter. I confess I was fishing as to your marital status."

"I see no purpose in your curiosity, Reverend. But as you've requested, I forgive you."

He smiled. "You're most kind. And as to my curiosity, I suppose my purpose is simply that I've watched you most of the day. I saw you take Mr. Spencer's daughter in hand. It's obvious that you are a woman of quality with a capable hand. Those would certainly be the qualities of a parson's wife, don't you think?"

Grace's jaw dropped at his audacity. She watched speechless as he tipped his hat and rode away. Straightening her shoulders, she replayed the scene in her head. Surely the reverend was joking. He wasn't seriously suggesting that he wanted to marry her, was he? It had certainly appeared that way.

She still mulled the question over in her mind when she realized the wagon in front of her had stopped. Yanking on the reins, she glanced around for Bobbin. The girl was nowhere to be seen. With an inward groan, she realized she'd been so distracted that she'd lost track of the child. Panic enveloped her as her mind raced back to another child for whom she'd been responsible and whom her ineptness had caused to come to harm.

Setting the brake, she wrapped the reins and hopped down as quickly as her skirts allowed. She ducked around the oxen and moved to the outside of the wagon train. As she spotted Bobbin, her heart caught in her throat. The child was crouched down by one of the wheels on Miss Turner's wagon. A lit fuse in her hand, her arm poised to toss the firework. "Bobbin, don't!" Grace called, but it was too late, a rapid release of explosions lifted into the air. The oxen started, with Bobbin still by the wheel as the wagon lurched forward.

The little girl's scream pierced the early evening sky.

&

Paul's heart caught in his throat at the sound of a child's cry. His mind became a jumble of thoughts as he raced toward Miss Porter's wagon. Judging from the obvious sound of fireworks and Grace's hollered words, he had no choice but to assume Bobbin had carried out her earlier efforts that had been thwarted.

A crowd had settled around Miss Turner's wagon. His heart lurched at the sight that greeted him. Miss Porter sat on the ground, Bobbin gathered in her arms, still as death.

"Is she. . . ?"

Miss Porter looked up, her face white. She shook her head. "She fainted from the pain. I think her leg is broken," she said, her voice shaking.

Paul turned his gaze to Bobbin's unconscious face. "Bear, go for Jonas."

"I'm here," Jonas said, hurrying up next to him. He took hold of Bobbin's trouser leg and ripped until her twisted, bruised leg was revealed.

A collective gasp lifted up from the onlookers. Jonas turned. "Okay folks, break it up. I need two boards, and some bandages. Who can get me those?"

One of the men had some boards he'd planned to mark the name of his ranch on once he built his homestead. But he said he reckoned this was the use the Almighty had intended all along. "I'll be back directly," the old-timer said.

"I have a sheet I was about to rip up for rags," Mrs. Clyde offered. "Might as well use it to help splint that leg."

"Thank you," Jonas said. "Will you bring a blanket as well?"

Mrs. Clyde elbowed her way through the crowd. "All right," she said. "You heard what the man said. Break it up. Go about your business, and let these folks take care of the little girl."

Paul turned to Miss Porter. "What happened?"

"I was speaking to the reverend and lost track of her for a few moments." She dropped her gaze and rested her chin on Bobbin's head. "I'm sorry, Mr. Spencer."

Paul stooped down next to her and placed his hand on her shoulder. "Don't blame yourself."

She lifted her tear-filled eyes to his. "It was completely my fault. I shouldn't have allowed myself to become distracted by a gentleman. Had I performed my duty as I promised, the child would not be injured."

Jonas cleared his throat. "I'm going to have to lay her down on the ground so I can set this leg." He turned to Paul. "Can you hold on to her, or should I have one of the other men help?"

Feeling the blood drain from his face, Paul took a deep breath. "I'll hold on to her."

Nodding, Jonas reached for the child, but Miss Porter held on tighter. The woman was clearly more fragile than all other indications. "Give her to me, Grace," he said.

Without a word, she loosened her grip. Bobbin moaned, but thankfully, she remained unconscious as Paul laid her on the blanket.

Grace moved back and stood.

Paul glanced up at her as she turned her back and slowly walked toward her wagon, her shoulders slumped. He'd speak with her later, try to reassure her that Bobbin would find her own trouble no matter how closely she was monitored.

Mrs. Clyde returned with several lengths of material. "I cut the strips. Use as many as you need," she said. "Land sakes, that's a bad one. You know what you're doing, young man?"

Jonas nodded. "I helped the surgeons during the war. Set all kinds of broken bones."

Mrs. Clyde shrugged and gave a sniff. "You don't look old enough. But that's neither here nor there." She nodded.

"Well, my Mr. Clyde was a doctor for forty years. I'll be right here to help you just like I did him, God rest his soul."

"That's most likely for the best." Jonas looked at Paul. "Let Mrs. Clyde help."

Paul sat back on his heels, resting his palms on his knees, and allowed Mrs. Clyde to slide her ample form between him and Bobbin. When Jonas took hold of the girl's leg, Paul turned his gaze from the limb to the child's face. He swallowed hard as the sickening sound of a bone cracking into place reached his ears. Bobbin cried out in her unconscious state, then went limp once more.

Reaching forward, Paul ran his hand along Bobbin's hair, fingering her braids, and the pink ribbons which, surprisingly, remained in place.

Jonas released a breath. "That ought to do it. We need to get her to your wagon and lay her flat."

"I'm not sure our wagon is the right place for her. The boys get awfully rowdy without me there to corral them." Not for the first time, Paul regretted his position as leader of this group of travelers.

"What about Miss Porter?" Jonas asked, lifting his gaze to the clearly distraught woman, hanging back. "Didn't Bobbin spend the day with you?"

Paul's stomach jumped at the thought. If she'd remained on-site while Jonas set the leg, she might have spoken up and volunteered her wagon and her services to help nurse the child.

"I'm not sure—"

"Don't be silly. Of course Grace will be happy to keep the child." Mrs. Clyde's insistence didn't raise Paul's confidence that Miss Porter would share her view. But he was grateful for the dowager's next words. "I'll speak to her." With a grunt, the woman lumbered to her feet, stumbled as she gained her footing, and nodded. "I'll be back."

Jonas looked at him frankly. "I'd suggest Pa's wagon, but I don't think Melissa's the type to nursemaid a child."

Paul nodded agreement. He didn't point out that the way Bobbin apparently despised Jonas's sister, it wouldn't have been a good idea anyway. The best choice was clearly Miss Porter, who despite her persnickety demeanor, seemed to have a way with children—at least with his children.

As if conjured by his thoughts, the three boys raced forward. "Uncle Paul!" Elmer ran into his arms, fat tears rolling down his freckled cheeks. "We heard about Bobbin. Is she dead?"

"No. She's just unconscious. She broke her leg."

"Do you want me to help get her to the wagon?" Bear asked. His solemn face seemed five years older as he focused on his little sister.

"We don't think it'll be a good idea for her to stay in the wagon."

"Why not?" Lester asked.

"Because I have too many duties away from our camp to look after her."

"We'll do that, Uncle Paul," Elmer said. "I could sit next to her and keep her company."

Lester nodded. "We'll take turns."

Paul smiled. He knew the offer came at the high price of staying cramped inside a stuffy wagon all day instead of running alongside the oxen in the warm, early autumn air. "That's good of you, boys."

Their faces lit up, and he almost hated to continue, but it was for the best. Bobbin needed an adult's supervision, preferably a woman. "I think it would be more fitting if Bobbin stays with an adult."

"Who?" Bear asked, his eyes filled with concern.

"Miss Porter is my first choice."

Relief passed over all three faces. Elmer nodded. "Bobbin

won't mind that so much."

Lester stuffed his hands in his front pockets. "You reckon Miss Porter will mind if we come and visit?"

Honestly, he had no idea whether Miss Porter would mind or not. "I can't speak for Miss Porter, but I don't see why she would mind an occasional visit. As long as you don't make nuisances of yourselves."

Bobbin moaned, drawing the attention of the men in her life. "Uncle Paul?" Tears ran down her cheeks. "My leg hurts."

Paul knelt beside her, placing his hand on her head. "I know it does, baby. The wagon wheel broke your bone." He thanked God that the leg was snapped instead of crushed. Hopefully it would heal properly and she would regain its full use.

The sound of crunching grass captured his attention, and he turned his head to find Mrs. Clyde returning. From the dark look on her face, he had to assume Miss Porter hadn't agreed to the request.

Mrs. Clyde shook her head. "Mr. Spencer. I have concluded that the child would be better off with me. After all, I helped my husband in his practice for forty years. I have plenty of room in my wagon."

Lester scowled. "We want Miss Porter."

"Hush, Lester," Paul admonished. "If Mrs. Clyde is offering to make room for Bobbin, then we will gratefully accept her offer."

Elmer scowled, and the normally sweet child kicked at the ground. "Bobbin won't like that. Why can't she stay with Miss Porter?"

Mrs. Clyde nodded, apparently not a bit offended by the lack of enthusiasm. "Miss Porter has other things to do." She looked at Elmer askance and offered a tight smile. "Don't worry, young man, I'll take good care of your sister. You may come and visit her any time you wish."

The news brightened the child's countenance somewhat, but Paul could tell he wasn't completely convinced. Still, Miss Porter must have her reasons. Paul met Mrs. Clyde's gaze. "We appreciate your generosity, ma'am."

Waving away his gratitude, she walked toward Bobbin. "She's still unconscious?"

"She was awake for a minute," Paul said. "She must have slipped back into unconsciousness."

"It's no wonder. The pain will be extensive." She released a breath and planted her hands on her large hips. "Let's get her moved before she awakens again."

"Is there anything to be done for the pain?" Paul asked.

Mrs. Clyde leaned close and spoke low. "I have laudanum in Dr. Clyde's medical bag. But don't let that information out. I don't have much, and we'd best save it for the worst of cases."

Paul nodded, relieved to know Bobbin would have the medicine to help with her pain, which he could only imagine must be excruciating.

He lifted Bobbin and followed Mrs. Clyde. The wagons had been circled, the oxen hobbled and let out to graze. From all over camp came the sounds and smells of evening meal preparation. Miss Porter glanced up from her fire as they passed her camp, but she quickly averted her gaze.

Swallowing his disappointment, Paul kept moving. Miss Porter obviously wanted nothing to do with them. He would respect her wishes.

six

Grace thought her heart might beat out of her chest as Paul walked past carrying the unconscious child. Three solemn boys trailed behind him. Thankfully, they didn't stop and speak to her.

With a guilty sigh, she finished warming the beef stew Betsy Mae had sent. After cutting a slice of bread from a loaf, she settled on the ground, her back pressed against the wagon wheel, and closed her eyes in silent prayer. Before she said *amen*, her mind went back to Bobbin, and she prayed the little girl would make a full recovery.

When she opened her eyes, Elmer stood looking silently down at her, his eyes asking questions for which she had no answers. Or at least no answers she could give. How could she tell the boy that her incompetence had been the reason his sister was hurt? And that Bobbin wasn't the first child to suffer due to her negligence?

"Elmer? Can I do something for you?"

She steeled her heart for whatever was coming.

"How come Bobbin can't stay in your wagon?" he asked through a gap where his two bottom teeth had once been rooted.

Swallowing, she squared her shoulders against his sweet charm and honest question. "Because Bobbin isn't my child, Elmer. I have my own duties to attend to on our journey."

"She wouldn't be much trouble. She can't move around much." His eyes widened. "I could even stay with her to help you out. With water and food and things like that. You reckon?"

"I'm afraid not, Elmer. It's not possible."

Disappointment washed over his face, and he averted his gaze until the blue eyes rested on her plate. His tongue flicked across his lips. As much as she'd rather he move on, Grace realized with all the confusion of the day that the child probably hadn't had his evening meal. If memory served, the family had planned to take dinner with Miss Turner, but after Bobbin's shenanigans, the young woman had claimed a case of nerves and had disappeared inside her wagon. Her younger sister, Valerie, had built their fire, and Grace could only assume that Melissa wouldn't be much help. Mr. Spencer's brood would likely go hungry or be forced to eat a meager fare.

"Are you hungry?"

Elmer lifted hopeful eyes. "Yes, ma'am."

"Miss," she gently corrected and handed over her plate. She patted the ground next to her. "Sit here and eat."

"That's yours."

"It's okay. I haven't touched it. Besides, there's plenty more where that came from."

He took the plate but hesitated before taking a bite. "What about Bear and Lester? Maybe I shouldn't eat without them."

"After you finish eating, I'll help you carry the leftovers back to your camp."

His face split into a grin. "Yes, ma'am!"

Pushing to her feet, Grace shook her head. Some battles weren't worth waging, and apparently Elmer would never be able to wrap his mind around the fact that she was a *miss*, not a *ma'am*.

Taking another plate from the back of the wagon, she dipped some stew just as Lester and Bear walked by, noticed their young brother, and stopped. "Good evening, boys. How is Bobbin doing?"

"Sleeping," Bear replied, his eyes accusing even as his

tone remained duly respectful. "Mrs. Clyde gave her some medicine."

"Good."

Lester glared at her and then turned the same hostile glance to Elmer. "Why are you eating her food?"

The little boy's eyes clouded. He swallowed hard. "I was hungry."

"We got some biscuits at our camp. She don't want us around."

Grace remained silent, allowing the scene to play itself out. Elmer jerked his chin. "She gave me her plate. We was bringing you some."

Lester swiped a glance at the plate, and only a slight swallow gave away his desire for the aromatic stew.

"All right, that's it. Sit down, both of you. You may eat here tonight. I have much too much food for myself, and I'd rather give it to you than leave it for animals."

Bear hesitated. "You don't have to feel obligated, Miss Porter. Like Lester said, we got food back at camp."

"I never feel obligated to do anything, Bear. I'm giving you the food because I have more than enough and, with Bobbin's accident, no one has had a chance to prepare a meal at your camp. It's a reasonable solution." Grace finished dipping stew into the plate in her hand, and set a slice of bread to the side. "And it's the right thing to do."

She handed the plate to Lester. The child kept his hungry gaze on the food but folded his arms across his chest. "I don't want it."

"Fine," Grace replied and lifted the plate toward Bear.

He took the food. "Thank you, Miss Porter."

Lester scowled at his brother as though he were staring into the eyes of a traitor.

"Lester, I'll get you another plate if you'd like."

"No, thank you." He walked away, shoulders squared, arms

swinging like a soldier.

Grace couldn't help but admire his resolve. There was something to be said for taking a stand for a righteous cause. According to Lester, her decision not to take Bobbin in had made her a betrayer. His sense of justice wouldn't allow for retreat or backing down.

Grace filled another plate for herself and filled one for the boys to take to Paul, though the action might have been considered forward. Taking a seat on the tongue of her wagon, she tried not to allow herself the luxury of enjoying the feeling of feeding the boys. As a teacher, she'd always been partial to boys, ornery ones in particular, so long as their unruly behavior was a result of excess energy and not a result of a rebellious nature.

Elmer wasn't ornery, though, and Bear was the sensitive, intelligent type. He probably loved to read. Her thoughts went to the bag of books behind the wagon seat. No, she would not offer him one to read. She must not become attached to these children.

"When you are finished eating, please set your plates on the ground next to the wash basin," she said to the boys. "I must leave camp for a few minutes."

"You didn't finish eating, Miss Porter," Bear observed, nodding at her plate. "Are you sick?"

"I'm fine, thank you. It's been a long day. I'm not very hungry."

"Can I have some more, Ma'am?"

"Elmer!" Bear growled. "You know better."

Grace nodded toward the pot hovering above the fire. "It's all right. There is more than enough. The stew won't keep for another day, so please feel free to eat as much as you'd like. And take that plate for your uncle. If you'd like, fix another one for Lester when you go."

"Thank you, Miss Porter."

Tossing her shawl around her shoulders, Grace walked away from her wagon toward the creek. Within a few minutes, she had settled against a tall oak rooted along the soft bank. Alone with her thoughts, the events of the day washed over her, overwhelming her senses. Only the knowledge that she couldn't give way to her struggling emotions kept her tears at bay. She leaned her head back against the rough bark and closed her eyes. How could she have been so negligent again?

This journey was supposed to be all about putting past mistakes behind her and forging a new life in a new world. A new position. And now she was repeating the same lapse in judgment that had gotten another child killed only a year earlier. Thank heaven Bobbin's injuries wouldn't kill her, but that didn't salve Grace's guilt one bit. The child had been left in her care, and because she hadn't been paying attention, had been hurt.

God had to be telling her something. Or punishing her.

She stayed at the bank of the creek until she thought the children had been given ample time to finish their meal and leave her camp.

Trudging back to the camp, she mentally prepared for the rest of the night. Clean up, douse the fire, and stretch out under the wagon, praying that sleep would come and give rest to her guilt-ridden mind.

≈

Paul gave a weary swipe of his forehead with the back of his hand. How could a day that had begun with such promise end with such a terrible accident? Poor Bobbin still slept, and Mrs. Clyde had assured him that she would keep the child pain free, which Paul translated as sedated, for the next couple of days during the worst of the healing process. For that he was grateful.

"Hey, Uncle Paul," Bear said as he approached the fire.

"Want some coffee?" Lester asked.

"Thanks, son." Paul ruffled the boy's sun-bleached hair. His stomach rumbled; then he remembered supper. How could he forget to feed the boys? Curled up on a bedroll under the wagon, Elmer slept. Paul glanced at the fire, but there was no sign that anyone had done any cooking. The boys must be famished. It was surprising that Lester hadn't rustled anything up for them. But he couldn't fault the boy. "Give me a few minutes to drink my coffee, and I'll round us up something for supper."

"No need," Bear said, nodding toward a crate next to the wagon. "Miss Porter sent some food for you and Lester. Me and Elmer ate at her campfire."

Paul raised his brow. "She did?" Grateful, he walked across the camp and took one of the plates. He held the other out to Lester.

"I ain't eating her food, Uncle Paul."

"She do something to offend you, Les?" Paul knew how stubborn the boy could be. He'd have to tread carefully if he was to get Lester to eat a bite, and the fact was that he couldn't keep up tomorrow on the trail if he didn't get some food in his belly tonight.

"You know she wouldn't let Bobbin stay in her wagon."

That was a puzzle for Paul to solve. He settled on the ground, pressed against a wagon wheel, and looked at Bear. "You feel the same way?"

Bear gave a shrug. "I guess I wish she would've kept Bobbin. I don't rightly understand why she wouldn't. She seemed fond of Bobbin and the rest of us, but then she didn't want to help out. But I ate." He grinned.

Lester shook his head. "I can't figure why she wouldn't help us out, Uncle Paul, can you? Like Bear said, looked like she liked Bobbin a lot."

"Whatever her reason, Lester, Miss Porter had the right not to get involved." He swallowed down a bite of stew and pointed at the other plate. "You ought to eat up, son. Tomorrow is going to be a busy day. You'll need your strength."

Lester hesitated, and Paul recognized the hunger in his eyes. But the lad shook his head. "We got some biscuits leftover from breakfast and lunch."

"Suit yourself, then."

Bear rose and stalked to the plate. "If you're not eating it, I'm going to."

Paul waited. If anything would get Lester to change his mind, the threat of his brother eating his food would do it. But the boy remained firm in his commitment to principle. Bear shrugged and dipped into the stew.

Paul had never felt so weary. Grateful for the nourishment, he ate the cold stew with relish. He could only pray the next day wouldn't be as challenging as this one had been. After finishing his meal, he plunged the dishes into a basin of water and cleaned them. He turned to Bear. "I'll be back."

"You taking those to Miss Porter?"

"I'm sure she'll be needing them."

"What for?" Lester asked, the scorn still edging his voice. "She's all alone. Don't seem like she'd need more than one plate and one fork."

"You're getting close to insolence, Les. I suggest you simmer down about Miss Porter and stop being disrespectful."

He mumbled an apology, but the fire never left his blue eyes.

"Now," Paul said, "you two douse the fire and pack up everything we won't need in the morning. Then you can roll out your beds and turn in."

"Yes, sir," they answered as one.

Paul's stomach tightened as he approached Miss Porter's camp. But as it turned out, his nerves were for nothing, for she was nowhere to be seen. Dirty dishes sat on the ground by the wash basin. Apparently Miss Porter had gone for a walk. It was pretty clear the dishes belonged to the boys. He weighed his options. He could either leave the two plates he'd brought and go back to the boys, or he could clean up the mess made by the children under his care.

His ma's reminder about good manners reverberated through his memory, dictating his answer. There didn't really seem to be a choice. Rolling up his sleeves, he lifted the plates from the ground and plunged them into the cool water. Glancing at the fire, he noticed a kettle hanging from a hook above the pot of stew. At the very least, it would be warm. He took the kettle, confirming the warm liquid inside, and poured it into the wash basin. It did little good, but it couldn't be helped. In a few minutes, the dishes were washed. He debated whether to dispose of the stew, but decided against it. Miss Porter might be planning to keep it for another meal. Although, he'd advise against it, if he were asked.

He hesitated, surprised at how much he wished Miss Porter would arrive and take a few minutes for conversation with him. He truly wished to learn the reason for her sudden aloofness. After a couple of minutes, he started feeling like a fool. He had his nightly rounds to make. With such a small wagon train, he preferred to do so on foot. It felt more personal that way.

His first stop was at the Turners'. Valerie, the fifteen-year-old younger sister of Melissa and Jonas, was alone. She had obviously just finished cleaning up after their dinner, a dinner he and his children had originally been asked to share. He understood why Melissa would be upset, but he couldn't help but take notice of the fact that she hadn't stayed earlier to find out if Bobbin had been hurt. Her lack of maternal instinct, or at the very least common concern for a child who had been hurt, perplexed him.

Valerie looked up when he approached. She offered a timid smile. Paul noticed the alarming difference between the two girls. Each was as pretty as the other, but Valerie seemed an unassuming sort, Melissa quite forward. She was the sort of young woman his sister would most likely have labeled *fast*.

"How is the little girl, Mr. Spencer?" Valerie asked.

"The wheel ran over her leg and broke it."

Even in the light of the fire, Paul could see her eyes widen with horror. "Oh, Mr. Spencer. How awful for her. I'm just so sorry."

"Valerie!" Melissa's insistent voice rang from the wagon. "Where is my tea?"

"Coming, Mel," she called back.

Melissa's head appeared through the canvas flap. "Well hurry up, for heaven's sake." Her brows pressed together in frustration until she saw Paul. Then the lines smoothed out, and her dimple flashed as a pretty smile replaced her frown. "Why, Paul, did you come to check on me?" She reached out. "I vow I must look a fright. It's been such a trying day."

Paul stepped up dutifully and took her hand, helping her from the wagon. "How are you holding up, Miss Turner?"

She gave a shaky breath. "I've been distraught to tell you the truth. Can you imagine if the oxen would have bolted with me in the wagon? Why, I could have been killed. I've been distressed all day at the very thought."

"Melissa," Valerie said quietly, "Bobbin broke her leg."

Melissa turned a haughty gaze on her sister. "Bobbin?"

"My niece."

"Oh." Melissa gave a wave as she settled onto a crate next to the wagon. She seemed unaffected as she adjusted her gown to billow about her legs. Paul glanced away as a white flash of lacy petticoat peeked through.

Valerie frowned. "A broken leg, Mel. Do you know how much pain that little girl is in?"

"Well, she should have thought of that before she set off fireworks."

"Melissa! Think about what you are saying. Have you no heart?"

Paul stood in stunned silence. He searched for an acceptable exit because he might just give in to his urge to explode his frustrations on this selfish young woman. Staring at her with her lips pinched, her brow squeezed into a frown, he couldn't believe he'd ever thought her beautiful.

Even now, she jerked her chin at her sister. "I do have a heart, but the child has been nothing but hateful to me all day. Now I am supposed to feel sorry for her because she received justice?" She turned to Paul. "I mean, I didn't wish the harm on her. I'd never, ever do that. And it's not like she's going to die, is she?"

"She'll live." Paul set his lips in a firm line.

"Well, then, you see? I have nothing to feel sorry about. After all, I'm the victim in this scenario. It could have just as easily been me with the broken leg."

"If you'll excuse me," Paul said, "I best finish my rounds before turning in."

"I'll be over to see Bobbin tomorrow, Mr. Spencer," Valerie said.

"That's kind of you. But she's staying in Mrs. Clyde's wagon while she heals up. And she'll likely sleep through the first few days." He refrained from mentioning the laudanum. "But after she's more alert, I'm sure she'd welcome some company."

"Mrs. Clyde?" Melissa's mouth twisted with amusement. "I'm surprised she's not staying with Miss Porter. You know she has her cap set for you, Paul."

Her pout wasn't nearly as beguiling as it had been just hours ago.

"I doubt that, Miss Turner."

"Why else would she have volunteered to keep that horror of a child all day?" She smiled broadly. "Oh, but I suppose that is the reason you aren't allowing your niece to stay with her."

"I don't understand what you mean."

"Oh, come now, Paul. The woman was supposed to keep the child from getting into trouble. Obviously she failed to do so. It's her fault I was almost killed and the little girl was hurt."

"I'm afraid I don't see it that way at all." But he had a feeling maybe Melissa had put her finger on some truth from Miss Porter's perspective. Was Grace blaming herself?

"Oh, but Paul. . ."

Valerie stepped forward at just the right moment. "Didn't you want some tea, Mel?"

"Yes, thank you," she said, more graciously than Paul had observed in the girl so far. "I can only hope it will calm my nerves so that I can sleep tonight." She sent Paul a truly pathetic look. "I can't tell you how I've been shaking since the incident."

Paul used every ounce of discipline he possessed to keep his voice steady. "I'm sure you'll be fine tomorrow."

"Oh, I hope so."

Paul nodded toward both women.

Valerie sent him a sympathetic smile. "Please tell Mrs. Clyde I'll be around to help with Bobbin as soon as she is ready for company."

A genuine smile found its way to his mouth. "She'll appreciate it, I'm sure." He lifted a hand in farewell. "Good evening, ladies."

"You're leaving already, Paul?" Melissa said. "I thought you came to see me. Couldn't we go for a walk or something?"

"I'm sorry. I have to check on all of the wagons. Then I have a meeting with the men." A meeting he dreaded. The first day hadn't gone well by anyone's standards; and even if his niece hadn't been the cause of the trouble, he would have been held responsible since he was the wagon master.

Melissa scowled at the news, but accepted his words more graciously than he'd anticipated. "Perhaps you can stop back by after your meeting and say good night?"

"I'll see what I can do."

The picture of her satisfied smile lingered in his mind as he walked away, heading toward the Adams' wagon, which was next in line. He was greeted by the bark of their dog and a smile from the shy, slim Mrs. Adams who, unless Paul missed his guess, was in the family way. Why hadn't he noticed sooner? And why would Mr. Adams allow his pregnant wife to make the journey west in this condition?

"How is Bobbin?" she asked.

Paul repeated the news of Bobbin's condition and where she would be staying.

Mrs. Adams nodded. "It's good to have Mrs. Clyde with us."

"I take it you'll be in need of whatever services the wife of a doctor can offer?"

She ducked her chin. "It's that obvious?"

"'Fraid so."

"Don't tell Jeremiah."

"Your husband doesn't know yet?"

She shook her head. "He thinks I'm plumping up." Her eyes twinkled. "Said the walking on the trail ought to do me some good. But he don't really mind. His ma was a heavy woman."

"I won't tell." He filed the information to the back of his mind. He had to admit he was glad Mrs. Clyde was along. Even with Jonas's experience patching up men during the war, he most likely didn't have experience delivering babies.

With a wink and grin at the two young children peeking out at him from behind their ma's skirt, he moved on until he'd seen to all of the wagons. Everyone seemed to be faring well at the end of the first day. Mercifully, the incident with Bobbin appeared to be the only real problem.

By the time he trudged back to his camp, most of the campfires were out except for the main fire kept by the night guards, and folks were settled in for their first night on the trail. He only prayed the next morning would bring a better day.

seven

This wasn't the first time Grace had been here. At least it felt familiar. A ramshackle cabin in the middle of a clearing in the woods. Mist swirled about her gray, muslin skirt as she walked slowly toward the foreboding dwelling, illuminated only by a barely discernable sliver of a moon. Her legs slid through the thick fog as though she walked thigh-deep in a quagmire.

Though she tried to stay quiet as she stepped onto the platform, her heels boomed on the wooden planks, echoing through the air like the sound of cannon fire. Her hands shook as she reached forward and grasped the leather latch on the door. She pushed. Her heart pounded in her chest as the door opened with a groan.

Placing one shaking leg in front of the other, she entered the musty, dark, one-room cabin. The soft sound of a child's whimper reached her ears. "Hello?" she whispered.

The whimper came louder.

"Are you there?" she whispered again, lifting her voice into the air with more force.

"Help me, Miss Porter."

Sammie?

Her heart shot to her throat. "Where are you?"

"Over here."

Grace tried to lift her leg to move forward, but her body seemed stuck.

"I'm coming, honey," she said, trying to keep her voice from shaking.

"I'm scared."

"It'll be okay. I'm coming."

The door flew open and a hulking shadow burst through. It floated past her as though unaware of her presence. A child's scream sliced through the darkness.

"Mama!"

With a jerk, Grace awoke. Pain slammed into her head as she sat up from her pallet beneath the wagon. With a groan, she grasped her head and slowly lay back down.

"Mama!"

Sam? She gasped. That was no dream. In a flash she slid from her bedroll and stood, dizzy from the sudden movement. She shook her head, waiting for her vision to clear. No, it couldn't be Sam. But it was definitely a child's cry. She listened more closely.

"Mama!"

Bobbin? As her mind regained clarity, she whipped around. Instinct drove her legs toward Mrs. Clyde's wagon.

Bobbin's cries grew louder. The drawstring on the canvas flap was untied. Grace pushed it aside and peered into the wagon. Mrs. Clyde sat beside the frantic child, trying to console her. Bobbin's arms thrashed about.

"What's wrong?" Grace asked.

Mrs. Clyde struggled to keep Bobbin still. "Land's sakes, Miss Porter. Come in here and help me before she does more damage to her leg."

Grace climbed into the wagon and crawled forward. "What happened?"

"She woke up, and when she didn't recognize her surroundings, she began to scream. I can't calm her."

Instinct took over. "Let me try."

Mrs. Clyde moved around Grace and climbed from the wagon as Grace turned her attention toward Bobbin. "Shh," she said. "You've got to calm down now."

To Grace's surprise, Bobbin settled down and stared up at her with wide eyes. "My leg hurts." Her lips quivered, and tears rolled down her cheeks.

"I'm sure it does. When you scared the oxen, the wagon wheel rolled back onto your leg and broke it." She waited for her news to sink in; then she proceeded. "Mrs. Clyde was kind enough to offer you a place to stay in her wagon. She also has medicine that will make you feel better."

"If you'll pass me that black bag, I'll get her another dose ready."

Grace did as Mrs. Clyde asked, then turned her attention quickly back to the little girl.

Bobbin stared up at her with wide, pain-filled eyes. "Where's Uncle Paul?"

"I'm here."

Grace turned to find Paul standing outside the wagon looking in. Suddenly she became aware of her hair, loose and flowing down her back. "She was. . .uh. . .crying."

"I heard," Paul said. "I think the whole camp heard her."

"It hurts, Uncle Paul," Bobbin said.

"I know, honey."

Crawling to the opening in the canvas, Grace hesitated as Paul reached out to help her down. She placed her hands on his shoulders and allowed herself to be lifted from the wagon. Time stopped as he set her on the ground, holding her so close they almost touched.

"I'll leave you to care for her." Grace stepped back, and Paul dropped his hands from her waist.

His eyes remained locked with hers. "Thank you for coming. It means a lot."

"I didn't do anything."

"Don't listen to her," Mrs. Clyde said, coming upon them suddenly with a bottle and a spoon in her hand. "I thought the child would beat me black-and-blue with all that flailing about. She didn't calm down until Miss Porter sat next to her and started talking."

Grace's cheeks warmed as she met Mr. Spencer's gaze. "I suppose I'm more familiar to her than Mrs. Clyde since she spent the day with me."

Her words conjured the memory of exactly why the child was in this situation in the first place. And condemnation tore at her heart. "I best let you get to her."

"Good night, Miss Porter," Bobbin's frail voice called out. "Will you come back tomorrow?"

Grace glanced back inside the wagon. She opened her mouth to promise the child anything—the moon, or at the very least her presence tomorrow. But she stopped herself short of agreeing to such a thing. "Good night, Bobbin. I pray you feel better soon." She turned to Mr. Spencer, who still stood too close for comfort. "Good night, Mr. Spencer."

His eyes were clouded in disappointment. "Thank you again, Miss Porter."

Nodding, Grace turned away. Aware of his gaze upon her, she forced herself not to look back. How could it be that in only one day, this man and the children in his care had already found their way into her heart? Shaking her head, she squared her shoulders, determined not to allow her emotions to rule her good sense.

❧

Bleary-eyed and bone weary, Paul called for the wagon train to move out the next morning. Bobbin had made him promise not to leave her even after she fell asleep. He couldn't very well refuse her request. So he'd sat up all night, sleeping only when his head rolled, jerking him awake. Thankfully, the laudanum had done its work, and Bobbin had slept through the rest of the night. She'd barely moaned when he pressed a kiss to her forehead before daybreak and left Mrs. Clyde's wagon, ready to face the second day on the trail.

By the time their lunch break was over, the sky had grown dark, and a heavy rain fell. But that didn't stop the travelers.

They chose to press on and trudged forward, the oxen and horses flinging mud as they worked their way along the trail.

Paul kept a watchful eye on Bear and was gratified to notice that the young man was plenty capable to drive the oxen and care for his two younger brothers.

Twice, he'd checked in on Bobbin. Mrs. Clyde assured him the child had woken only long enough to eat a few bites. She also assured him the canvas cover was plenty secure enough to keep out the rain so he didn't have to worry that Bobbin would get wet and risk becoming ill.

Paul had tried not to think about the way Miss Porter felt in his arms the night before when he'd helped her from the wagon, or how her hair had appeared, flowing freely past her shoulders and resting just past the curve of her back.

Finally, when he couldn't banish her from his thoughts, he made a decision to speak with her at the first opportunity. There was a logical solution to his situation, and he had every intention of seeing that solution through. He had no idea why Grace would have pulled away from the children so suddenly, unless it was as he had suspected—that she felt the guilt of Bobbin's condition. But he would reassure her that no one blamed her for the mishap.

A slice of lightning followed by an explosion of thunder effectively brought the wagon train to a halt two hours before he'd planned, but Paul was encouraged. They'd traveled fifteen miles that day despite the foul weather and muddy ground. Hopefully, if the rain ended soon, they would get the same amount of miles in tomorrow, too.

But the rain continued for two days, the ground growing muddier by the hour, it seemed. The animals were having an increasingly difficult time pulling through the sludge; and finally, after the Adams's wagon became bogged down in the mire and broke an axel, while the men worked to get it unstuck, Paul called a halt until such a time as they could move forward without potential damage to any of the other wagons.

Without the benefit of fire, meals consisted of dried meat and hard biscuits or bread the ladies had brought from home—something that they would do without until they reached the fort and the women once more had access to an oven.

On the second evening of the halt, with no end of the rain in sight, Paul pulled his collar up and forged through the mud until he reached Miss Porter's wagon. She was nowhere to be seen, so he stood outside the drawn canvas. "Miss Porter?" he called.

In seconds, she appeared. A tentative smile curved her lips. "Is everything all right, Mr. Spencer?"

He nodded. "I just. . ." Suddenly at a loss for words, he wasn't sure how to continue, so he said the first thing he could think of. "Bobbin asked for you."

Frown lines appeared between her eyes. "She did?"

"Well. . .no."

"I don't understand."

Rain was beginning to trickle down his neck, making the situation even more miserable. "I guess I just wanted to find a reason to speak with you."

"I'm sorry, Mr. Spencer, but you're not making any sense."

Releasing a heavy breath, Paul felt like a complete fool. He wished he'd have thought things through a little better. Miss Porter gave a shiver as the rain dripped into the wagon.

"I'm sorry to have bothered you, Miss Porter," he said. "I reckon I don't have anything to say, after all."

Miss Porter peered closer at him, her eyes suddenly widening. "Are you certain, Mr. Spencer? I assure you I will not be offended by anything you have to say."

Paul's heart raced. Did she know what he wanted to ask? Was she open to the idea?

"I just wanted to say. . ." He swallowed hard. "I think the children like you quite a bit."

Her eyes clouded with caution. "Yes."

He chided himself. Of course she wouldn't want him to bring up the children first. Even if they hadn't known each other more than a few days and love wasn't a factor in his suggestion, any woman in her right mind would want some sort of assurance that he had tender feelings toward her at a time like this. But folks married for different reasons, and there was an attraction between them. Surely she wouldn't be able to deny that.

Out west, women were scarce, or so he'd been told. Now would most likely be the time to secure a wife for himself if he had any chance at all of finding a suitable partner for building a new life.

Backtracking, he wiped the rain from his neck with a wet hand. "I shouldn't have started that way. What I meant to say. . ."

"Mr. Spencer. May I interject?"

When he'd finally gotten the nerve to speak? He swallowed hard, wishing the rain would stop pouring over his head and down his back. "Go ahead."

"I have been expecting a visit from you for several days. I assumed the foul weather had delayed our conversation."

"Oh?"

"I know it must be difficult for you to confront. So rest assured, I blame myself entirely for Bobbin's accident. Nothing you have to say on the subject will offend me." Her lip quivered, whether from emotion or cold he wasn't sure.

She thought he blamed her? Paul opened his mouth to protest, but she gave him no chance. "I assure you, I alone am to blame for allowing my attention to be diverted by the reverend's visit."

Oh, was that what she thought? "Miss Porter. That's not what I was going to say."

"I know you're too much of a gentleman to blame me to my face, but I wanted you to know you don't have to be kind to me or even civil. I'll do my best to keep to myself for the rest of the journey. But you must ask the children not to come to me as they tend to do."

"They're fond of you."

"I can't imagine why."

"Because you showed them fairness instead of telling me they needed a firm hand like everyone else they've crossed since their ma and pa died. You've fed them and somehow even got Bobbin to brush her hair."

She waved away the last comment. "Bobbin wants to be a girl; she just doesn't have anyone to encourage her in that direction."

Paul swiped at the rain on his face once more. "And that's exactly what I wanted to discuss with you."

The confusion didn't leave her eyes, but a hint of a smile curved the corners of her lips. "Then perhaps you'd better get to the reason for your visit, Mr. Spencer. I fear you're about to be washed away in this rain."

He gave a nervous sort of chuckle. "I reckon you're right about that."

She waited while he formulated the words.

Finally, Paul gathered a breath and decided just to blurt it out. "I—well, it seems as though you have a way with children. And with you being a woman alone and all, and me being in need of a wife. . .well, we'll be at Fort Laramie in a few weeks. . .and. . ."

A gasp left her as her eyes went wide with. . .was that horror?

Paul's courage failed him, and his words faded.

He stared into Miss Porter's blue eyes, wishing they were looking back at him with tenderness, softness. He'd always dreamed that beautiful eyes like hers would look on him with affection, even adoration if he was being honest.

"Mr. Spencer, your proposal is very kind, and I appreciate the thought that went into your words." She hesitated only a split second. "But God hasn't seen fit to find me a husband all these years. And. . .I am not. . ." She seemed to struggle with the next words. "I am not meant to raise children."

"I don't understand. You're wonderful with children."

A short laugh burst from her throat. "There's a little girl with a broken leg a couple of wagons away who might disagree with you."

"I don't hold that to your account, Miss Porter. Even if you don't want to marry me, you should know that no one blames you for Bobbin's accident." He couldn't help but laugh. "I'm surprised she hasn't broken an arm or a leg before now. Some children you just can't control. The second a person turns his back, she's into something else that could hurt her." Paul inwardly cringed. If he had any chance at all of her changing her mind, telling her things like this about the children wouldn't help his cause.

"She is willful," Miss Porter said, nodding. "But that's not necessarily a bad thing. Whoever becomes her mother will need to help steer her in the right direction, that's all."

"And you don't think that woman could be you?"

Averting her gaze, she shook her head. "I have a house-keeping position waiting for me in Oregon City. I'll be head housekeeper in a new and elegant hotel. So you see, even if I were so inclined, I couldn't possibly get married and leave my friend without help. I've given my word."

"I assumed you were headed for a teaching position."

"No. I stopped teaching because I was tired of raising other people's children. So you see. . ."

And suddenly he did see. She didn't want to be bothered with Bear, Lester, Bobbin, and Elmer. She had her own life to tend and didn't want anyone interfering with her plans.

"Well, I suppose I should get out of this rain. It wouldn't do for me to come down sick and further delay the wagon train."

She nodded. "Thank you for the offer, Mr. Spencer. It was kind of you to think of me. If I may be so bold, I believe Miss Turner would be pleased to accept such an offer from you."

"I'll keep it in mind." He tipped his hat. "Good day, Miss Porter."

"Good day, Mr. Spencer."

Feeling as though the wind had been sucked out of him, Paul trudged through the mud back toward his wagon. His stomach tightened at the thought of what might happen if they weren't able to reach Fort Laramie before the snows began. They were cutting it close as it was. October was just about over, and November marked the beginning of winter weather.

As though the heavens responded to his thoughts, the rain began to beat down in pellets of ice. By the time he reached his wagon, sleet was beating down.

There was nothing to do but crawl into the cramped wagon with the shivering boys and wait it out.

eight

By morning, the sleet turned to snow, and snow was easier to maneuver than mud. Still, the pioneers shivered as they moved forward inch by inch. By the end of the week, the sun finally came out and the temperature rose enough to melt away what had fallen and to dry the ground.

Grace stayed to herself as much as possible. An occasional visit from Reverend Ellis eased her loneliness. Though she knew he was looking for a wife just as well as Mr. Spencer was, she tried to enjoy his company without leading him to believe she would welcome a proposal of marriage.

When the sleet and snow had begun, Grace had chalked up her foul mood to the cold. But within a couple of days, she realized, she missed the children. They went by often on their way to visit Bobbin. Lester still glared, but Elmer gave her a sad little wave as he passed. She would love nothing better than to gather him up onto her wagon seat and ask him to recite his ABCs. Or tell her how his day was going. But he was so like. . .Sam. Every time she thought she might relent and allow the children access to her heart, she remembered the little boy and steeled herself once more against an onslaught of guilty shame.

At times, she could put the entire situation out of her mind, as the terrain grew rockier the farther they traveled and the oxen harder to handle. Luckily, the snow held off, and the temperature remained bearable, if a little chilly. By the time the wagon train reached Chimney Rock, the band of travelers was back on schedule and eagerly looking toward the end of the next three weeks, when they would arrive at Fort Laramie and begin the process of waiting out the winter.

In honor of reaching Chimney Rock, Mr. Spencer called a halt for the day, even if it was only noon. Four men went hunting, hoping to get a deer or elk—something to roast for tonight's feast. Grace had decided not to make the trek up the rock to see the natural structure up close, as most of the folks were doing. She searched for buffalo chips, built a fire, and walked to the river to draw water. By the time she returned to camp, it was all but deserted except for Mrs. Clyde and the reverend, along with a couple of men who had remained to guard the camp.

"There you are," Reverend Ellis said, taking the pail of water from her hand. "I came to escort you to the rock."

"That's kind of you," she said, unable to keep from smiling. "I hadn't planned to go."

"Hadn't planned to go?" He pressed his hand to his chest in mock horror. "Surely you don't mean that. This is a once-in-a-lifetime opportunity. They say if you stand at the bottom and look up, you can't even see the top of the rock."

"He's right," Mrs. Clyde called from her fire. "If I didn't have this bum hip, I'd be hightailing it over there myself."

"How is Bobbin doing?"

"That child?" Mrs. Clyde gave an exasperated wave of her hand, as she limped over to Grace's fire. "She's already getting herself into trouble just sitting next to me on the wagon seat. I vow it'll be a mercy to get that child mended and able to walk again. No child with that much energy was meant to be denied a chance to burn some of it off." Her words might have sounded exasperated, but she spoke with the hint of a smile and a lilt in her tone.

"It's a shame she can't go see Chimney Rock."

"Oh, she went. Paul and Miss Turner took her." She grinned. "The child looked just like a monkey hanging off his back that way." She sniffed. "That Turner woman was clinging a bit herself."

Grace felt just a hint of outrage that Paul had moved on so quickly. It had only been a little over a week since he'd asked her to marry him. "I'm surprised Miss Turner was interested in the venture, considering her animosity toward Bobbin."

"Oh, I think all that is water under the bridge. That woman doesn't have enough sense to hold a grudge. If you ask me, I'll bet we'll be attending a wedding not long after we arrive at Fort Laramie."

Not all of them would be attending a wedding. The old woman could bet on that if she wanted. "Don't you agree, Grace?" Mrs. Clyde asked.

Grace gave a shrug. "It's really none of my affair whether he marries her or not," she said, trying to put the image of Miss Turner as the blushing bride out of her head. Even though she'd suggested the woman to Paul, she couldn't stop the twinge of jealousy. Under different circumstances, she most likely would have accepted his proposal herself. Of course, if he didn't have those children to raise, he would never have asked her in the first place. Not her, when he had a beautiful young woman such as Melissa Turner to turn his head with her seductive smile and tight dresses outlining every curve.

She shook the image from her mind and turned her prettiest smile (which unfortunately wasn't even close to one of Miss Turner's dimpled smiles) to Reverend Ellis. "I'd be happy to accompany you to the rock, Reverend. Give me a couple of minutes to freshen up a little first."

He flushed with pleasure, making his round face redder than normal.

"I'll be waiting right here."

Mrs. Clyde kept the reverend company while Grace prepared for the trip. She took a cloth and wiped away some of the trail dust, and secured the pins in her hair so they wouldn't fall out during the trek up the rocky trail.

In just a few minutes they found themselves walking toward the landmark, Grace's hand firmly in the crook of the reverend's arm as she listened to his plans for the future. His excitement for sharing the gospel was genuine and something Grace couldn't help but admire. His passion reminded her of the way she once felt about teaching children. There was something about speaking into their minds and helping impart knowledge that they would never forget. That, she had always believed until last year, would be her legacy. Perhaps some of her students would grow up and remember her as one who had influenced their current ideals. It was a lofty goal, to be sure—the thought that she would have that much to do with any child's future.

"I hear there are camps of Indians just outside the fort," he said. "Friendlies, but not yet converted. I am looking forward to the opportunity to share the gospel message with them."

"You truly love what you do, don't you, Reverend?"

"A man should find joy in his labor according to King Solomon, writer of the Ecclesiastes."

"What about a woman?"

He stared at her as though she had asked the most foolish question possible. "Why, a woman should find joy in her home, husband, and children, of course. That is her heritage as helpmeet to a man. It's why she was created in the first place."

"What about women whom God has chosen not to allow to wed?"

He stopped and turned to her, looking down on her with a tender smile. "I don't think you have anything to worry about, my dear. You may be starting late in life, but I have a feeling God is most definitely listening to the cry of your heart."

"The cry of my heart?"

"To make a suitable marriage." He continued to look at her as though she were the youngest, most endearing of children.

Grace stared at him in horror. "Reverend Ellis, I was not hinting at a proposal."

"Of course you weren't, my dear." The amusement in his tone belied his words.

"I am serious." Grace took a breath. "I have a position waiting for me when I arrive in Oregon City. A very good position that I am very blessed to have. I'm not looking for marriage. And I do not want children."

A frown creased his brow. "Is this true, or are you simply being coy for my sake?"

Grace smiled. "Reverend Ellis, I would not know how to be coy if I tried. I am not well versed in how to employ women's wiles."

"Why I know that," he replied, obviously flustered. "Forgive me if I implied that you would stoop to manipulation to procure a proposal of marriage."

"You're forgiven." Grace motioned toward the rock. "It appears as though everyone is returning. Should we continue so as not to arrive back at camp after dark?"

"Yes, of course, we wouldn't want to take that chance."

If they arrived after dark, she would be compromised and therefore most certainly expected to marry the reverend—something she did not wish to do. He was a nice enough man, but after hearing his views on a woman's place in marriage, she wasn't sure she wanted to be his helpmeet. As a matter of fact, she was almost positive she wouldn't be satisfied in that position at all.

To be sure, a woman should care for her husband, home, and children, but there had to be more. Even the excellent woman in Proverbs 31 bought and sold land. She used her mind and did so with her husband's full support. Grace wasn't foolish enough to believe that a farmer's wife could have both, nor a rancher's wife. But what of a lawyer or doctor in a city? Was there a more forward-thinking man to be found in the city?

"Shall we go?" she asked.

He hesitated, then nodded. "Certainly."

They met the others coming back, everyone chatting and laughing, few saying hello to Grace. Not that she could blame them. She'd held herself aloof since Bobbin's accident, speaking to people only when necessary.

Her heart jumped when they met Mr. Spencer, Miss Turner, and Bobbin on the trail. Melissa gave them a wide smile, her fingers tightly wound around Mr. Spencer's arm.

Even Grace had to admit she was beautiful, her eyes bright with excitement, her face flushed with the cool wind and sun.

Bobbin waved, grinning broadly.

Grace's heart softened at the sight of her, but she knew how little encouragement it took to win over a child, and she didn't want to give the girl false hope. So she gave a quick nod and swept past without looking at Paul.

Bobbin didn't seem to take the hint. "Miss Porter!"

Drawing a deep breath, Grace stopped and turned. The trio had turned, and Grace could feel Paul's accusing glare on her. She refused to look him in the eye. "Yes, Bobbin?"

"Are you going to write your name on the rock?"

"I guess not. I didn't bring anything to do so."

"I have some charcoal left over." She stretched out her dirty hand.

The gesture threatened to break through Grace's defenses.

Melissa's timely interruption renewed her resolve. "Now, Bobbin. Miss Porter doesn't want that dirty thing in her hand."

Bobbin jerked her chin. "She does, too."

Her disdainful tone was an indication that Melissa may have won over Paul Spencer, but Bobbin wasn't so easily manipulated. Still, Grace didn't want to chance Bobbin growing fond of her again. A year earlier, nothing would have kept her from taking that charcoal and making Bobbin feel like a heroine from a novel for offering it. But that was all in the past. From now on, Grace couldn't risk her heart. She wanted nothing to do with children. It was just too risky.

She gave Bobbin a steady look. "Miss Turner is correct. I don't want to dirty my hands. Thank you, anyway."

"But I know you want to write your name on Chimney Rock. You said so."

"You're mistaken," Grace said firmly, trying to remember a conversation where Bobbin might have gotten the impression that she wanted to write her name on Chimney Rock.

"Yes you did," Bobbin insisted.

"Bobbin." Paul's voice was firm. "Don't contradict Miss Porter."

"But she did say she wanted to write on the rock. Remember when you put the ribbons in my hair?"

Grace relented beneath the child's insistence. "Remind me," she said softly.

"My ma used to tell me about Chimney Rock and how we would write our name on the bottom. And you said—"

Grace nodded. "That it would be nice to know that all the folks to come after us would read my name, and that even if I had no children to carry on my name, I would never be forgotten."

Bobbin nodded.

"But I wasn't talking of Chimney Rock. I was speaking of Independence Rock. Remember? I said I'll climb up on the rock and find a place where no names were and I would carve out my name and the year I was born."

A bright smile split the child's face, and she nodded. "I remember now. Maybe by then I can climb up with you."

Grace couldn't bring herself to say no, so she averted her gaze. "Perhaps," she murmured.

"Let's go, Bobbin," Paul said. "Miss Porter wants to be on her way."

"Miss Porter, do you want to take the charcoal and write your name on Chimney Rock, anyway? I did and it was fun."

As if drawn against her will, Grace's gaze turned to Paul. He looked back at her, his eyes tender and reflective. Grace swallowed hard and lifted her gaze to Bobbin. "No, thank you. Like I said, I'd rather not get my hands dirty."

She turned, but not before seeing the disappointment cloud Bobbin's face, and a scowl mar Paul's nearly perfect face.

"Shall we go?" she heard Melissa ask.

The reverend cleared his throat. "Well, let's continue."

Grace took his arm once more, and they stepped toward the rock. While he spoke of his dreams for the future, she found her mind wandering back to Bobbin and the look of disappointment on her face. By the time they reached the rock, the reverend was wrapping up his diatribe.

Grace found herself scanning the names written at the base of the enormously tall rock.

"May I ask a question, Miss Porter?"

"Of course." Reluctantly she turned her attention from the rock.

"Do you have feelings for our wagon master?"

Feeling exactly like cold water had been tossed in her face, Grace was speechless.

"I can see by the look on your face that I've shocked you. I'm sorry for speaking out of turn."

"I. . .no, that's all right."

"No, I had no right. I can only attribute my lack of sensitivity to an appalling tendency to be jealous."

"J–jealous?"

"It can't have escaped your notice that I spend more time with you than any other single woman on the wagon train."

"Well, yes, but. . ."

"And I must admit that it hasn't escaped mine that you spend more time with me than anyone else. I find it to be flattering."

Mercy, the man had an ego that could not be pleasing to the Lord. She had half a mind to remind him that pride goeth before destruction.

He took her hand and stared at her with earnest appeal. His voice softened. "But more than flattered, I find myself imagining ways that I may convince you to become my wife. And I know you were not hinting at a proposal before we were interrupted, but you must know that possibility is something I have been contemplating since the first day of our acquaintance. I find myself wanting to find a way that I could possibly deserve a woman of your intelligence, warmth, and kindness. You would do me a great honor if you could look past my inadequacy and become my wife."

Grace had read accounts of how quickly men and women grew acquainted and decided to marry while on the trail west. But she hadn't expected it to happen to her, not once, but twice in just two weeks. She, Grace Porter, the spinster schoolmarm, now being treated like the belle of the ball. This had to be a dream.

"Your silence isn't very reassuring, my dear." His attempt at levity fell flat on Grace's ears, and his chuckle sounded eerie.

"Reverend Ellis," she began.

"Please call me Christopher."

Grace smiled. "I didn't know your name was Christopher. How can I marry a man whose first name I didn't even know?"

He pulled her forward, pressing the back of her hand against his heart as it remained clasped in his.

"Say yes, and I will tell you anything you would like to know about me."

Grace's eyes scanned his face. There was no question that he was sincere. His was a good strong face; his eyes smiled when his mouth turned upward. Certainly he was not a handsome man, but neither was he unpleasant. She wasn't sure of his age, but from the gray temples and lines around his eyes and mouth, Grace would guess him to be in his forties. That alone wasn't enough to keep her from marrying him. Many men married younger women, particularly if their first wives had passed away.

If it were simply a matter of finding a reasonably pleasant-looking man who was good-natured and kindhearted, the reverend would be an acceptable choice for a husband. But that wasn't enough for Grace.

"Christopher," she said softly, gently pulling her hand from his. "You do me a great honor by asking me to marry you."

He cocked his head to the side. "Somehow I have a feeling you are not building up to accepting my request."

"I'm afraid not."

"I'm not very eloquent, but is there anything I can say that might change your mind?"

"Nothing that I can think of." Grace couldn't help but smile. "I do not share your passion to share the gospel."

He frowned. "Surely you know that we are all called to share our faith." His tone held just a hint of reprimand.

"Oh, I know you're right," Grace agreed, nodding. "I just meant I don't feel called to become a missionary. I am not ashamed of my faith when God opens doors."

"I apologize for my abruptness." He drew in a breath and expelled it with force. "I tend to become frustrated with my brothers and sisters in Christ. At times, it feels as though I am the only one who cares whether or not the heathen are brought to a saving knowledge of Christ."

"I assure you, Reverend Ellis, I do care, and I would be most happy to help in any way I can while I am at Fort Laramie, but I do not consider preaching to the Indians to be my life's calling."

"Then perhaps you are right to refuse my proposal." The smile he offered her appeared to be genuine, and Grace found herself responding.

In the distance, she heard the sound of excited whooping coming from the wagon train. "I wonder what the excitement is about."

The reverend glanced toward the wagon train. "Unless I miss my guess, I'd venture to say the hunters have been successful. I suppose that means we will have a feast tonight."

Grace's stomach growled at the thought. "I'll look forward to fresh meat after all the smoked meat we've been forced to endure during the bad weather."

He nodded. "I can almost taste that roasted meat now."

They seemed at a loss for conversation now that the proposal had been presented and rejected. Grace decided to take the lead. She slipped her hand through his elbow. "Shall we return to camp? I should really find out where I can be most useful in helping with the meal."

"Yes. Good idea." He seemed relieved with the plan, and they barely spoke during the ten-minute walk.

He left her at her wagon, tipped his hat, and said good-bye.

Grace shook her head. She had lived twenty-three years believing herself to be too plain to attract a man, but apparently men in the west or those thinking ahead to the west weren't so choosy about looks. For the first time in her life, she had something of value to offer a man, and all it took was her presence and the lack of a husband to pique interest. A smile played at her lips. Apparently, any wife was better than no wife at all, and because men in the west outnumbered women by a large margin, there was a mad dash to secure a woman before the competition widened.

"What are you grinning about?" Mrs. Clyde's voice drew her from her thoughts. "You musta had a good time with that preacher."

"I had a very nice time. It was good to stretch my legs."

"He didn't look too happy walking away from here. I figured you two must've had words."

Her observation stole the smile from Grace's lips. "No. We didn't have words exactly."

The dowager nodded, her eyes flashing with understanding. "He asked you to marry him, did he?"

Grace felt her jaw drop. "Why, how on earth did you know?"

"It's obvious. The way he's been hanging around your wagon, strutting away like a peacock. But this time he walked away with his head hung like a whipped pup."

"Well, I certainly never encouraged him."

Mrs. Clyde narrowed her gaze. "Why'd you turn him down? You know you're not likely to get a better offer."

A lot she knew. Grace was tempted to tell her about Mr. Spencer's proposal in the rain. But she thought better of it. The very idea of such a handsome man proposing marriage would most likely seem like an embellishment to Mrs. Clyde, and Grace wanted to relish the memory, not have it tainted with skepticism.

A shrug lifted Grace's shoulders. "I don't know. I suppose I don't want to be a preacher's wife. That's all."

"Well, it's just as well. The man is old enough to be your pa." She patted Grace's arm. "If I was a betting woman, I'd wager the good reverend will have himself a wife before we pull out of Fort Laramie in the spring."

Heat rushed to Grace's cheeks at the thought that she was so easily replaced in a man's affections. The image of Melissa Turner clinging to Paul's arm and looking up at him with adoring eyes reduced her memory of his proposal to what it was. He wanted a mother for those four children, and she had seemed the best choice for that role, given how quickly the children had taken to her.

As if by providence, she heard Melissa's laughter and turned to the sound. Sure enough, Paul stood with the girl, grinning like a fool, surrounded by her brother, Jonas; her pa; and her sister, Valerie. Along with Melissa's family, Bobbin was hanging from Bear, who seemed to have eyes only for the pretty younger sister. Lester and Elmer stood on the edges of the group looking miserable.

"Oh honey." Mrs. Clyde once more pulled her from her thoughts.

"What?"

"You're wearing your heart all over your sleeve. That's what."

Jerking her head, Grace turned away from the happy little group and added chips to her fire. "Did you keep this going while I was gone?" she asked. Buffalo chips were only good to keep a fire going if they were constantly fed into the flames. As long as she had been gone, there shouldn't have been anything left but a memory.

"Nope."

"No?" Strange. "It must have been higher than I remember."

"Nope."

"Mrs. Clyde, are you being intentionally cryptic?"

The woman smiled as if she knew a secret. An annoying smile, if Grace had to put a name on it.

"It's just that Mr. Spencer came by and built the fire up once, and his boy Lester came over once."

Grace opened and closed her mouth three times before she found her voice. She turned and stared back to the little group. "I wonder why he would do such a thing."

"Yes, it is a mystery, isn't it?"

As if summoned by her stare, Paul turned and found her gaze. Grace caught her breath and couldn't look away.

Even Mrs. Clyde's short laugh couldn't pull her from the warmth of Paul's eyes.

"Yes," Mrs. Clyde repeated. "It's quite the mystery."

nine

The smell of roasting meat raised everyone's spirits. For the first time during the almost two-week trek, the folks in the wagon train seemed ready to celebrate. And as much as Paul would have preferred to keep moving forward, he knew that for the sake of morale he should take Jonas's suggestion for half a day's rest at Chimney Rock. For the next three weeks, they would continue on without delay. Barring inclement weather or any other unavoidable problems, they would be at the fort sometime in mid-December. At least, they'd spend Christmas in the safety and warmth of the fort.

They could expect to wait out the winter and move out about April, which would put them several weeks ahead of the next wave of wagon trains leaving Independence, Missouri. That was good for them. Unclaimed land was becoming scarcer since the end of the war just two years past. The country was filling up with displaced Southerners who either had seen their homes burned or were facing property taxes at a rate meant to send them in disgrace from land that had been in most families for more than a hundred years.

Paul was determined to stake his claim before the west became too crowded for comfort, but for now, he had other things to deal with. Bobbin's need to stop being carried around on either his or Bear's backs, for one thing. He had been working on a gift for her, and now that she was healing and back at his own camp, he planned to give it to her as soon as she and Bear returned from the creek, where he had insisted all the children go and wash up before the celebration.

Along with roasted meat, the camp was beginning to smell

of other things. He detected the aroma of fried corn mush, which they would eat with preserves. A couple of the women were attempting to bake cakes over the open fire. Even if they weren't perfect, he knew folks would appreciate the treats. Even cornbread soaked in molasses would be served. His mouth watered at the thought.

But first things first. Mr. Leonard Sands had requested—no, demanded—a meeting with him. Paul's gut clenched as he watched the man strutting toward him. He could tell by the set of his jaw and the determination in the man's eyes that he wasn't happy. Bracing himself, he prepared for the man's complaint.

"Right on time, I see, Mr. Sands."

"A man's only as good as his word," came the gruff reply. One that Paul should have anticipated, considering the man's typical demeanor.

"I agree. What can I do for you?" Normally, Paul would have offered a cup of coffee to anyone who had made an appointment to see him, but he was hoping to keep this meeting brief. He stayed on his feet and didn't offer Mr. Sands a seat on one of the pickle barrels Bear had set out for use during the celebration tonight.

"It's my girl, Matilda." Tilly Sands was a sweet seventeen-year-old girl. Paul had thought more than once that she'd be pretty if she'd straighten her shoulders and look a person in the eye every once in a while; but her pa was hard on her. Paul had seen it more than once and worried that the man's temper might get the better of him one of these days.

"Something wrong with your daughter, Mr. Sands?"

"Nothing you can't take care of for me."

"Oh? What can I do?"

"That scout of yours has been sniffin' around like a dog. I don't like it."

So that's why Jonas had been so happy lately. He had his

eyes on a young lady.

"Jonas is a good man, Mr. Sands. Matilda could do a lot worse."

A stream of tobacco juice shot from his lips into the fire. "No daughter of mine is goin' to make eyes at no Yankee."

"The war's been over for two years. I'm sure, if you try, you can find some common ground with Jonas."

Mr. Sands' face glowed red, and he shoved his calloused finger in Paul's face. "I ain't askin' your advice, Paul Spencer. What I'm sayin' is that Yankee best keep hisself away from my girl, or there's bound to be trouble."

"I see," Paul said, tight-lipped. "What do you expect me to do about it?"

"I expect you to take your man in hand and tell him to keep away from Matilda, or I'm goin' to plug him."

Paul peered into the man's eyes and had no doubt that he meant every word. He fought back a shudder of dread and lifted his chin. "Now you listen to me, Leonard Sands. I won't abide any violence in this wagon train. We discussed that there would be Southerners and Northerners alike on this journey. In the west, we won't be held by those titles. We're all going to be working together to build up the west—side by side. And if you cause any trouble, I'll be asking you to leave this group."

"So you ain't gonna say nothin'?"

"I'll speak to him and tell him about your objections, but I can't guarantee what he'll do. A man don't take kindly to threats. Especially when it comes to a woman he's taken with. I suggest you have a talk with Matilda."

"Believe me, I aim to." Something about his tone of voice raised Paul's suspicions and sent a ball of concern to his gut.

"One more thing, Mr. Sands."

"What's that?"

"As wagon master, I'm telling you, I'll not stand for a man beating on a woman."

"You tellin' me how to raise my own flesh and blood?"

"I'd say at this point, your daughter is a grown woman able to make up her mind about a man; but even if she weren't, I would put a stop to any man who raised a fist to a woman or child. Now I'm not saying I'd stop a reasonable thrashing like the Bible talks about. I think you know the difference."

Anger mottled his face. "I ain't gonna be told how to punish my daughter!"

"Let's just say you've been warned, then."

"I could say the same thing." He spun around and stomped away. Paul made a mental note to discuss the matter with Jonas. He would recommend that his friend stay away from the girl, but knowing Jonas, the cocky young man wouldn't be deterred by something as insignificant as an irate, threatening pa. At least, Paul would warn him to be careful and discreet. He had no doubt that Mr. Sands would follow through with his threat against Matilda despite Paul's ultimatum.

☙

Grace felt a flush of excitement the minute the music began and Mr. Adams grabbed his wife and whirled her onto the open space the women had made that would serve as a makeshift dance floor. No one cared that the dance floor was made of earth instead of wood. It was just so good to have some fun after almost two weeks on the trail, over half of which had been miserably wet or cold. There was a definite chill in the air, and everyone wrapped up in warm clothing, but the weather didn't deter many folks from the dance, other than the two women nursing babies. The reverend was notably absent from the festivities. Grace couldn't help but be a little disappointed. She hated the thought of being a wallflower.

But she needn't have worried. Jonas Turner stood before her almost immediately. "Care to take a spin around the dance floor with me, Miss Porter?" Hard-pressed to resist the handsome man's dimpled grin, which she had to admit was a lot like his sister's, she nodded and placed her hand in his.

She noticed Bear had shuffled up to Valerie Turner's side and was talking to her, obviously trying to drum up the courage to ask the girl to dance. Jonas noticed her gaze. He chuckled. "Those two are a little young to be courting, don't you think?"

"Perhaps." She grinned. "Although my grandparents were both sixteen when they got married. And my mother was fifteen when she married my pa. Of course, he was twenty-one, so that probably made them both seem more marriageable by the standards of the day."

Jonas's silence brought a flush of heat to Grace's face. "I suppose you didn't want to know so much."

Still he didn't speak. When he missed a step and trounced on her foot without seeming to notice, she ventured a glance at his face. His eyes were clouded over, and he stared somewhere beyond her. Turning, Grace saw a young woman next to an older man, presumably her father. She'd seen them before but had never spoken to either. The man appeared to be enraged. The girl ducked as he raised his hand. Grace stiffened and gasped. Surely he wouldn't. . .

"He'd better not," Jonas said through clenched teeth. "I'll kill him."

The man apparently came to his senses as he slowly lowered his hand and pointed toward a wagon. The girl turned and fled, then disappeared inside the canvas.

Pity rose in Grace's heart. The poor girl was unable to attend the dance.

Jonas was shaking—from rage, Grace suspected. "Come on," she said. "We don't have to dance."

"Thanks."

They walked back to her wagon. "Is she your girl, Jonas?"

"I hope so. Her pa lost both of his sons and a brother at

Gettysburg. He blames me."

"How is that possible?"

"Not only me. Anyone who fought for the Union. He won't allow me anywhere near his daughter."

"I'm so sorry. Hatred does horrible things to a man's heart."

"I'd take my chances if it was just me I had to worry about, but you saw how he almost hit her. The only thing that stopped him was that people are around. If I defy him and see her anyway, he'll take it out on her."

"What will you do?" She couldn't imagine this determined young man would give up so easily.

He shrugged. "What *can* I do?"

A smile touched her lips. "Well, whatever it is, don't get caught."

Jonas took a somber breath and nodded. "I won't. Believe me, I can't risk it."

His stone-cold expression sent a chill down Grace's spine. "Be careful, Jonas. Sometimes it's hard to know what a man is truly capable of until it's too late. If you push him, his daughter might be hurt a lot worse than you can imagine."

From the corner of her eye, Grace noticed movement and turned her gaze. Aaron Bullock swaggered toward her, his mouth twisted into a crooked grin. "May I have this dance?" he asked, his voice filled with good-natured arrogance. He was forty, if he was a day, and married to boot. "And where is Mrs. Bullock?" she asked.

"Dancing with the wagon master." He gave a hearty laugh. "Don't worry, Miss Porter, all I'm asking for is a dance. I got my hands full enough with my missus." He winked. "Yes, ma'am, I'm a happy man." Without waiting for her to answer, he nodded at Jonas, grabbed Grace by the waist, and twirled her onto the dance floor.

And so it happened. As soon as one man deposited her back at her wagon, another one took his place. For the first hour and a half, all the dances were lively, with very little touching between dancing pairs. When the waltzes began, her dance card seemed to empty pretty quickly. Apparently, the wives demanded the waltzes for themselves. Grace enjoyed watching the love spilling over between the husbands and wives. She was so caught up that she failed to notice Paul approach her until he spoke. "May I have this dance, Grace?"

Grace? She had never given him permission to use her name, but somehow it seemed fitting. She smiled. "I'd be delighted."

At the first touch of his hand on her waist, Grace gave herself to the beauty of the dance. They didn't speak, but he looked into her eyes as they danced. He didn't hold her too close. Still she felt incredibly close to him. So close, in fact, that she could feel the warmth from him radiating to her. She wondered if he felt the same but would die before she'd ask.

Disappointment tangled with relief in her gut by the time he took her back to her wagon. Elmer and Bobbin were there to greet them. Both grinned from ear to ear. "I told you Miss Porter would say yes, Uncle Paul."

"Yeah, Uncle Paul," Bobbin shot out. "You owe me an extra piece of Mrs. Bullock's cake."

For a moment, Grace had difficulty processing the meaning of their words. But it sounded like they were saying. . .

She lifted her gaze slowly to Paul. "You wagered with your children?"

He looked like a man sentenced to be hanged. "It wasn't quite like. . .that."

Grace turned to Elmer. "Why did your uncle ask me to dance?"

"'Cause I said, 'I bet Miss Porter will dance with you, Uncle Paul.' And he said, 'Aw, she don't want to dance with me.'"

Bobbin tugged on her sleeve until Grace looked down at

her. The child was barely balancing on a pair of hand-carved crutches. "And then I said, 'If she says yes, you have to give me an extra piece of cake.' And Uncle Paul said, 'And what do I get if she says no—which she will.' And I said, 'I'll be good for a week.' And so he said, 'You're on, little girl.'"

"And so he asked you, and you said yes, and now Bobbin don't got to be good and she gets an extra piece of cake." Elmer elbowed his way back into the conversation. He frowned and turned to Paul. "Uncle Paul? Do I get some more cake, too?"

"Go get some, both of you. Tell Mrs. Bullock I said it was okay."

Elmer took off at a run, slid to a stop, and came back. "I forgot," he told Bobbin as he waited for her to maneuver the crutches.

"It's not exactly like they said, Grace."

Drawing a breath so deep Grace thought she might never expel all the air, she looked him squarely in the eye. "Let me make this perfectly clear, Mr. Spencer."

"Grace, please. . .don't say something final."

"I would appreciate as little interaction with you and the children as possible. We will be at Fort Laramie in a few weeks, and it will be much easier to avoid one another then. In the spring, I will not journey on with this train."

A frown creased his brow. "What are you saying?"

"I am going to wait for the next wagon train to pass through. I will simply telegraph Hattie Beddington and explain my delay."

His eyes narrowed. "You're a stubborn woman, Grace. I've never known anyone to throw away happiness like you're doing."

"Happiness? I shall be very happy as a housekeeper to what is sure to become the most prestigious hotel in Oregon City." Oh, why couldn't he just go away and leave her alone?

"This is what you want? No man in your life? No us, Grace? Look me in the eye and tell me you didn't feel something when we danced."

Her heart raced as he stared down at her, his hand gripping her arm. "I—I don't know what you're talking about."

He released her, and the spot where his hand had been felt ice-cold. "You're a liar, Grace Porter. A stubborn woman and a liar to boot. Maybe you're not the right woman to warm my bed and raise my children."

Grace's mouth dropped open at his shocking words. Her hands flew to her cheeks as though she'd been hit, and she watched him walk away in a blur of tears. Whipping around, she hurried to her wagon and climbed inside, drawing the string tight. The tears fell as she spread out her quilts and ducked underneath.

She wept through three more waltzes until, slowly, the sobs subsided, and she steeled her heart against the memory of the hurt and anger on his face, the truth of his words. She'd felt something as they danced. Had wanted it to last. But he was the one who. . .he had made a fool of her by asking her to dance because of a wager, not out of a desire to hold her in his arms.

Only a few more weeks until they reached Fort Laramie. The only question was, Would her heart be intact when they arrived, or torn into a million pieces?

ten

Paul knew he was every kind of fool. And stupid to boot. Every day since that night at Chimney Rock, he regretted being sucked into a dare by those two gluttons. All they'd wanted was a piece of cake, and he'd fallen for it because, coward that he was, he needed the shove to gather the courage to ask Grace for a dance. He'd respected her wishes, stayed away. When he needed to give instructions, he sent Jonas to relay the message. He had thought she might come around before they reached the fort, but now, with only a day to go before they arrived at their destination, she'd stood firm in her resolve.

She did her fair share of the work, seemed to be taking her meals with Mrs. Clyde and the reverend on a regular basis. But she refused so much as to glance in his direction. It was as though she'd forgotten he existed.

They were practically at the front gate of the fort, and once they went inside, there would be no reason for her to suffer his presence. The thought of all those soldiers finding favor with her irked him. What if one of them proposed to her and she said yes?

He stiffened as anger flashed through him at the very thought. She deserved much more than being an army wife.

"Paul!" At the sound of his name on panicked lips, he glanced in the distance to find Jonas riding hard. Shoving aside thoughts of Grace until he had time to figure out how to talk her into forgiving him, he rode out to meet the scout.

Jonas pulled his mount to a skidding halt, tossing up dust. "We have big trouble ahead."

"Indians?"

Jonas shook his head, swallowing hard to catch his breath. "Blizzard. Headed this way."

Paul glanced to the west. How had he failed to notice the clouds rolling in? "How far off is the fort?"

"Five miles, but we'll never make it."

"We can't risk having these wagons stranded out here. We'll have to hunker down and give it a try. Tell everyone to get their children inside the wagons and to speed up the oxen. Get pots and pans out. Clang them together from the back of the wagon, so the wagon behind will know to follow in case it gets bad enough we can't see where we're going."

He nodded. "Anything else?"

"Yes, tell everyone to connect their ropes. Tie them from one wagon to the next."

"Are you sure? If one of us goes off in the wrong direction, everyone will be lost."

"No one will be lost." He spoke with a confidence he was far from feeling, but he had to try to keep the wagons together, and rope seemed the best way.

Jonas yanked the reins to do as he had been instructed.

"Jonas!" Paul called out. "Tell them to pray."

The wind picked up within a few minutes, followed by a few flakes at first. Then, as though the heavens opened, snow began to shoot from the sky—stinging shards of white.

"Stay close!" he called as he went up and down the wagon train. He stopped at his own wagon to make sure the children were inside with the canvas drawn to keep out the snow. "How are you doing, Bear?"

"I can't see my hand in front of my face, Uncle Paul," he called back. "Ain't no telling where we'd be if not for those pots and pans in front of us."

Paul was relieved he'd thought of it and attributed the idea to divine intervention. He was also relieved that their wagon had made the middle of the train in its rotation.

As the snow drove harder, he heard the sounds of pots and pans clanging less frequently, and he was even more grateful for the ropes tying the wagons together. Prayer spilled loudly from his lips as he dismounted and walked. Finally, he saw lanterns and heard clanging and yelling ahead of them. Jonas must have told the fort to be on the lookout for them.

Relief flooded over him like a warm summer rain. As they rolled through the gates of the fort, chaos ensued. The soldiers, tied to hitching posts against the blinding snow, helped put the animals in shelters and directed the folks into a large room that must have been a place for meals, for tables were set up and a large stone fireplace blazed. The wagon-train refugees flocked as close as they could to the fire. Paul didn't blame them. But first they had to take inventory of people and make sure no one was missing. He muscled his way through the crowd to the front and stood on the stone hearth. "Folks, we need to do a head count before we settle in too much. Men, count your family members and report back. Those of you traveling alone, please speak up for yourselves." So far he hadn't seen Grace. He was beginning to grow concerned.

"Mine's here," Mr. Adams called out. Mrs. Adams was pale and looked about dead on her feet.

"I don't have a man to count me, but I'm here," Mrs. Clyde called out.

"I'm here," the reverend offered. "Praise the Lord." Others murmured their agreement to his praise.

One by one, families were accounted for. Only one voice hadn't been heard. "Has anyone seen Grace Porter?"

Mrs. Clyde stepped up. "She was the last in rotation today. Behind the Bullocks if I'm not mistaken."

Paul felt rising trepidation. He turned to Aaron. "Who drove, and who clanged pots and pans?"

"I drove the oxen, of course," Aaron said, his demeanor a bit more humble than normal, due no doubt to the ordeal, but Paul had no doubt his swagger would return in the morning.

Mrs. Bullock looked white. She trembled, her face crumpled, and she dissolved into tears. "I didn't get the rope tied good. It must have slipped off. I didn't notice it until we got to the fort. If Grace is dead, I'll never forgive myself."

Paul stared at her, trying to digest the words. "You mean she's out there, lost in this blizzard?"

The question wasn't meant to be answered. Paul grabbed his saddlebag and headed for the door. "Bear, take care of the younger children. Make sure they have something to eat and get them to bed."

"Where are you going, Uncle Paul?"

"I have to go find Grace."

Jonas stepped forward. "You can't go out in this. You'll be killed."

"If I am, you'll have to get these folks to Oregon, come spring. Promise me you'll help Bear get settled on land they can call their own and keep an eye on him with the children. He's old enough to do it if he has to. I trust him to look after his brothers and sisters. But he might need some help."

"This is craziness, Paul. At least wait until the storm lets up."

"You know I can't do that." Paul clapped his hand on Jonas's shoulder. "Promise me."

A scowl spread across his face; his eyes grew stormy. "You know I promise. You're an idiot."

He looked up and saw Melissa approaching. He gave an inward groan. No matter how many times he hinted to this girl that he wasn't interested, he couldn't seem to make her believe he was serious. She was so used to getting her way that the thought that a man wouldn't fall at her feet and beg for her hand in marriage mystified her. She just couldn't seem to conceive of the possibility, so she simply chose to believe he truly loved her. Paul had even spoken to Jonas, who laughed and told him he was staying out of it.

"Paul," Melissa said, her eyes filled with question. "Where are you going? You can't leave. It's too dangerous."

"I'll be fine. One of the wagons didn't make it."

"Well, you still can't go out in a blizzard. You'll be killed."

"Don't waste your breath, Mel," Jonas said. "He's made up his mind."

"Who is missing?"

"Miss Porter."

Melissa rolled her eyes and huffed, her hands planted on rounded hips. "I vow she'll do anything to get your attention, Paul. It would serve her right if you left her all night."

"She could die if I leave her out in this."

"But if you go, you could die." Melissa's voice was soft and beseeching. Not her usual demanding stubbornness. Paul responded to the tenderness in her tone. He smiled. "I'm willing to risk it."

"Would you risk your life if I was the one out there instead of Grace?" Her lower lip quivered.

Jonas let out an impatient huff. "Melissa, leave the man alone. You know he'd come after you. Unless I could talk him into leaving you out there. Might do you some good to be buried in the snow for a day or two."

Sticking her tongue out at him, she took a swipe at him with the back of her hand. But he deflected it easily. Melissa turned quickly back to Paul. "Please be careful," she said.

She looked so young and vulnerable, that on impulse, he leaned and placed a kiss on her forehead. "I promise. You can pray for me."

Her eyes were filled with tears when he pulled back and met her gaze. "I will," she whispered.

Paul spoke with the soldier at the door, asking for directions to the stable where his horse was kept. The grizzled sergeant frowned. "You can't go out in this. It's a death sentence."

"One of my wagons didn't make it."

"You'll have to let them fend for themselves until the storm passes."

"Listen, Sergeant, I'm going one way or another. There is no them. The wagon is driven by a woman alone. I have to try to find her."

A frown creased the sergeant's face. "I see your point. I still say it's a bad idea."

"I can't help it." Paul waited, wondering if the sergeant would relent and not force him to barrel through that door like a battering ram.

"All right," he finally said. "There's ropes tied between the buildings. Turn right when you walk outside. The stable's the last building. Lucky for you, it's on the side of the fort or you'd never find it no matter how many ropes you hung onto."

"And where's the gate from the stable? Will there be a rope connecting the stable to anything after I get my horse?"

The sergeant expelled a heavy breath. "There's a rope stretched to the gate, but once you get outside these walls, you're on your own."

"I understand." Paul stepped past him. "Thanks for the help."

The sergeant placed a heavy hand on his shoulder, and Paul stopped just before reaching for the door. "You a praying man?"

"Yes, sir," Paul replied.

"Good. Me, too. I'll be praying you and the lady get back here alive and well."

Touched by the man's softened demeanor, Paul swallowed down a boulder-sized lump that suddenly rose in his throat. "I appreciate it."

A cold blast of snow and wind shot inside when he opened the door. He found the rope easily and closed the door. One hand on the rope, he used the other to raise his collar and hold it together at the throat in a vain attempt to keep the cold, stinging snow off his neck. His heart sank. The snow was coming down just as hard as earlier, maybe harder.

He looked ahead to a daunting task.

"Lord," he prayed. "How am I ever going to find her in all of this?"

Then as quickly as he prayed, the answer came. God's eyes were powerful enough to see through this storm. He knew exactly where Grace was—if she was wandering aimlessly on the plains, whether she was scared, or if she'd stopped somewhere and closed herself up in the canvas.

Paul hoped for the latter. If Grace had any chance at all of surviving, she'd have to sit still and wait it out inside the wagon. And that was only if her wagon remained sturdy against the wind. Paul tried not to think of the what-ifs. He especially banished the image of her being thrown as the wind knocked her wagon over.

The wind cut through him as he followed the rope. It seemed like hours before he finally reached the stable. Even through a heavy coat, sheepskin gloves, and a scarf, his body was chilled to the bone. Relief scored through him as he stepped out of the wind. He located Delilah easily. "Sorry, girl," he spoke as he grabbed his saddle. "I don't want to make you go back out in this crazy weather. But I need your help finding Grace."

Delilah nudged him, as though she understood and sympathized, as though she didn't mind going back in the cold wind and snow if it meant making him happy.

He led the horse outside. She pulled back at the first blast of wind, lifting on hind legs. "It's all right, girl," Paul soothed. "This is the hardest thing I'll ever ask of you. But we have to go now. We can't wait any longer."

Delilah settled down, ducked her head against the wind,

and pressed forward at his bidding. Holding on to the rope with one hand and Delilah's reins with the other, Paul reached the gate. No guard was on duty, most likely assuming it wouldn't be necessary given the violence of the weather. That was a mercy to Paul. He wouldn't have to have the same conversation he'd just gone through with the sergeant.

Paul kept a strong fist around Delilah's reins as he one-armed the wooden latch and opened the gate. He mounted, and horse and rider set off into a white night, striving against wind and snow, moving forward on a prayer and faith that God would lead the way.

❧

Grace wasn't sure when she'd realized there were no other wagons near her. Perhaps when the clanging of pots and pans ceased, but certainly when she felt around on the seat beside her, searching for the rope connected to the Bullocks' wagon. She'd yanked, only to discover no resistance. Her heart nearly exploded in her chest as her mind faced the truth: The ropes had come apart. She was all alone.

Ice-cold fear shot through her. She couldn't help it. Blinded, freezing, and alone. She knew how close death was unless she got back on course. But the swirling snow in front of her eyes was dizzying, disorienting. A heavy burst of wind shoved against the canvas, pushing the wagon. The oxen stumbled. A scream tore at her throat as the wagon tipped onto two wheels before settling back on all four. She knew she couldn't go any farther. The oxen couldn't see where they were going any more than she could. Her best chance for survival, small as it was, would be to unhitch the animals, hunker down inside the wagon, and pray that the blizzard ended soon.

Praying as she climbed down, she fought back tears of despair. There was no time; besides, her eyelids were freezing as it was. Icy tears would blind her even more. She felt her way along the wagon and eventually caught hold of the yoke.

Unable to maneuver the straps and hooks, she yanked off her mittens. Her fingers burned with cold as she unhitched the yoke from the wagon. She knew she couldn't allow the oxen to wander aimlessly on the plains, so she grabbed the yoke and pulled on it. As if by a miracle, the oxen cooperated and followed her lead as she turned them around. Feeling alongside the wagon with one hand, she led the pair to the back of the wagon, where she tied them to the axel.

Ducking under the oxen, she climbed into the wagon and pulled the drawstring tight to keep the snow from entering. She shivered, feeling the cold to her bones. She slipped on a second skirt and another shirt, then slid under every quilt in the wagon. Still her body shivered, trying to build its own inner fire.

Rolling onto her side, she pulled her knees up to her chest and waited, listening to the wind howl. She didn't know how on earth she would ever survive. If the canvas tore, she'd freeze to death. No one would be out looking for her. Even if the rest of the wagon train made it to the fort and realized she was missing, no one would be foolish enough to venture back out in a blizzard. The danger was much too real. Though she knew better, she couldn't help but wonder what would happen if someone decided to brave the storm to find her.

Against her better judgment, she closed her eyes, suddenly so tired she couldn't move. Was this how Sam had felt all those nights alone inside the cold dark shack before he was found?

Tears formed in her eyes and slid down the side of her face and into the crook of her arm where her head rested.

Oh God, is this my punishment for not saving him?

Her eyes closed. Suddenly she was back where the dream always took her.

eleven

Paul knew he was an idiot—the worst kind. He had left the safety of the fort on a fool's errand. He couldn't see Delilah's head, much less a lone wagon on the plains. Now the children would be left with no family at all except for each other. Still, he didn't bother turning around. What was the point? He'd never find his way back to the fort, anyway.

So he trudged on, Delilah barely moving as the wind shoved her along. Then as though in a miracle, the wind slowed down, the snow slowed until it barely fell. And he could see, not more than ten feet in front of him, a wagon. Nudging Delilah forward, he prayed harder than he'd ever prayed before.

❧

Grace saw little Sam on the floor, huddled against the wall. The hulking shadow stood over him, he looked up, terror on his beautiful little face, and he cried out. "Help me, Miss Porter! Miss Porter!"

"I'm trying, Sam." A sob tore at her throat. "I'm trying to get to you." But as though an entity unto itself, the ground held her fast. Her boots melted into the floor, and she pulled with all her might.

"Miss Porter!"

"Grace!"

A stinging slap startled Grace awake. She opened her eyes. Disappointment shook her. She was still dreaming.

Closing her eyes again, she tried to sink back into her dream. She had to get to Sam this time. She had to save him, if only in her dream.

"Grace!" Someone shook her. Frowning, she opened her

eyes again and stared into Paul's face. "Paul? You're not a dream?" she whispered.

Paul shook his head, his eyes misty and his smile genuine. "I'm real. You're safe now. The blizzard's over." He shook with cold.

"You're freezing."

"I'll be all right, now that I've found you."

Now fully awake, Grace sat up. "You have to cover up, Paul."

"Do you know what you're saying? This could cause trouble for you back at the fort."

"That's not important right now. What's important is that you don't die from the cold."

She was right. Paul knew he had no choice. His feet burned, as did his fingers and face. So he accepted the warmth she offered. She covered him, keeping one quilt layered between their bodies, the one attempt at propriety.

"You can't say no this time," he said, through chattering teeth and closed eyes.

"What do you mean?"

"You'll have to marry me. You've been compromised." He heard his words slur and felt himself drifting. His gloves were off, and he knew she was rubbing his hands, but he'd reached the place between sleep and wakefulness where he was unable to speak anymore.

❧

Grace worked feverishly while he slept. She wasn't sure she should have let him drift off, but awake, the pain in his swollen feet and hands would likely be unbearable. She had removed his boots and hung his socks up, hoping they would dry before he awoke. She slipped her hands beneath the quilts and rubbed and rubbed, trying to get the blood circulating in his toes. She couldn't guess how long he had been asleep. The sky outside the wagon was dark. Her arms ached from rubbing his hands and feet, but she couldn't allow him to lose any parts of himself because of her.

Her mind went back to his words as he had drifted to sleep, and her stomach jumped. He was right. She had no choice but to marry him now. She sat back in the darkness, pressed her face into her hands, and wept. He would expect her to mother the children. And she absolutely couldn't do it. She couldn't open her heart to another child. Bobbin's accident was proof of that. The guilt was too much to bear.

She awoke some time later to Paul shaking her shoulder. Her head jerked up. She reached up and grabbed at her neck, kneading the knots from her muscles.

Blinking awake, she stared silently into his eyes. "Why did you sleep sitting up?" he asked.

"Why do you think?"

"I see your point." He gave her a twisted grin. "But I should have been the one to do that."

She gave a shrug. "You needed to rest. How are your hands and feet?"

"They hurt." He took her hands and turned them over, looking down at her palms. "You probably saved them, you know?" His eyes shifted upward, taking away her breath with his grateful gaze.

"I pray so, Mr. Spencer."

"You called me Paul last night."

"I was half asleep and overcome with gratitude that you had come to find me."

"That's the only reason? I had hoped you might be starting to trust me a little."

Grace couldn't help but smile. "How could I not trust the man that came out in a blizzard to find me?"

"Good, then start calling me Paul."

"I'll try." Grace drew a breath, becoming uncomfortable with the intimate setting. She felt the canvas walls begin closing in. "Do you want me to get you some breakfast before we start toward the fort?"

He dropped her hands, giving her a short laugh. "I'm not sure we can get a fire built as high as the snow is. Do you have anything that doesn't require heating?"

Grace recognized his request as hopeful. They had not had supper the night before. He was most likely starving.

"I have some fried corn bread from night before last." She smiled. "Would you care for some of that? I have a jar of sorghum to dip it in."

"Sounds good." He moved toward the flap. "I'll wash up in the snow, and we'll get the oxen hitched. Good thinking, tying them to the back of the wagon, by the way."

Grace's heart thrilled under the praise. Her arms and shoulders ached until she could barely move from trying to get those animals from the front of the wagon to the back of the wagon. An acknowledgment of her forethought seemed to take away some of the pain and made it all the more worth the effort.

Paul untied the drawstring and climbed out. Within five minutes he was back, his face red from the cold.

Grace smiled as he returned. "That didn't take long. I take it you need my help to get the oxen hitched."

His eyes remained somber. No smile touched his lips. "Grace, there's something you should know."

Her stomach tightened. "What is it?"

"One of the oxen died in the night."

Unable to speak, she stared at him, her heart sinking as the words hit their spot.

"It. . .um. . .put its head down, presumably digging beneath the snow for the dead grass underneath." The expression on his face was one of misery. "I'm sorry, Grace. I think the snow must have frozen across his nose and mouth. It appears to have suffocated."

Grace shook her head. "I never thought to offer them some of the grain I brought with me. Why didn't I feed them?"

"During a blizzard? You had no choice but to get yourself inside to safety."

Grace closed her eyes, allowing his words to settle into her guilty brain.

"Not everything that happens is your fault, Grace." His quiet words hit her like a battering ram. She opened her eyes.

"What's that supposed to mean?"

He gave a shrug. "Only that anytime something bad happens, you take the blame."

"No I don't."

"You blamed yourself for Bobbin's accident."

"Only because I was supposed to be looking after her when she hurt herself. If I hadn't been distracted by the reverend, she would never have gotten hurt."

"Perhaps, or perhaps she would have simply done the same thing the next day while her brother should have been watching her, and maybe she would have been killed."

"That's not the way it happened, though. I was supposed to look after the child. My failure to do so almost got her killed."

"Anyone ever tell you you're one stubborn woman?"

"Yes. Just about everyone."

"Well, just about everyone is right. You are."

"I suppose we should butcher the ox and take it back to the fort. We can't let the meat go to waste."

"So this is where we are changing the subject."

"Only because there is nowhere to go with the previous one, Paul."

Besides, the quarters were becoming much too cramped.

Even in the freezing temperature, sweat poured from Paul as he labored over the dead ox, butchering the poor beast. Blood stained the snow, roiling Grace's stomach as she assisted him, cleaning the meat with the wet snow as best she could and storing the slabs inside an empty crate. Two hours later, after they cleaned themselves as well as they could, Paul hitched the other ox and mounted Delilah, as Grace took the reins. The snow had piled up as high as the top of the wagon wheels, and it took all of the remaining ox's strength to pull through the heavy drifts.

Grace's insides began to quiver as the gates to Fort Laramie came into view. How would she be treated when the folks discovered she'd spent the night alone with Paul? Of course, as a godly woman she'd made sure there was nothing improper in their conduct, but the situation itself gave the rest of the wagon train reason to suspect impropriety. Unfortunately, that was pretty much all some people needed.

Living a sheltered life in a Missouri prairie town, Grace had never seen an Indian. But outside the fort, an entire camp, evidenced by teepees and buckskin-clad braves, hunkered around campfires. She swallowed hard at the sight.

"It's all right," Paul said softly. "Don't be afraid."

"I'm not afraid." Not exactly. Besides, she was more worried about the folks inside than those outside.

Once inside, she was surprised to find so much activity with the blizzard barely over. It was so cold, all she could think about was getting out of her wet clothes and sitting next to a warm fire for as long as it might take to warm up.

Two soldiers took hold of the ox's bridle and led the wagon into a barn. Paul followed. When they were inside with the door closed, Paul dismounted and offered her his hand while she climbed down. Observing the merest of winces convinced her that his hands were still in pain from their exposure to the cold. "Is there a doctor at the fort?" she asked the young private who was tending the animals.

"Are you sick, ma'am?"

"Miss. And no, I'm not, but Mr. Spencer needs to have

his fingers and feet looked at to make sure he doesn't have frostbite."

"Our doctor was killed in an accident last month. Another one won't arrive until spring." He gave Paul a look of regret. "I'm sorry, sir."

"I'll live."

"Maybe Jonas could take a look?" Grace suggested. "If he worked with the doctors during the war, he likely has experience with frostbite."

Paul nodded. "You're probably right. I'll talk to him."

Mollified, Grace glanced around, unsure what was to be expected of her.

One of the soldiers seemed to notice her discomfiture. He inclined his head toward the door. "I'm to take you to your quarters."

"Thank you."

Paul offered her his arm. She slipped her hand inside his elbow, enjoying the warmth, but she noticed the way he hobbled. "Your feet are pretty bad off?"

"Nothing a few days and a hot soak won't cure."

"You sure?"

"Reasonably."

As much as she hated the thought of returning to the cold air, Grace nevertheless looked forward to settling into her quarters. A few moments later, the soldier stopped before a small cabin. Grace was grateful to note smoke escaping from the chimney. "You'll be sharing with four other women and a little girl."

Paul touched her arm and hung back as the soldier knocked on the door. "I'll talk to the reverend later today. Is tomorrow too soon for you?"

"Too soon for what?"

Paul frowned. "For us to get married."

"Oh, Paul. Let's not talk about that. I already told you, it isn't possible."

The door opened before he could respond, and Mrs. Clyde flew outside. "Thank the Almighty, He spared your life."

Under the maternal care, Grace fought the urge to burst into tears. "Paul found me."

"Paul?" Melissa Turner showed up at the door. She sped out the door and threw her arms around Paul's neck. "Oh, I'm so relieved you're all right."

Paul groaned aloud as the girl's booted foot stepped on his. "What?" Melissa asked. "Aren't you glad to see me?"

"Get off his feet, Melissa," Grace said sharply. She turned to Mrs. Clyde. "I think his feet might be frostbitten. I rubbed them trying so hard to get the blood flowing, but he's in quite a lot of pain."

"Pain is a good sign." Mrs. Clyde turned her attention to Paul. "Come inside, and let's take a look."

The soldier stepped between Paul and the door. "Sorry, sir, women only in the cabin for unmarried ladies."

Mrs. Clyde scowled at him, but he refused to back down. "I have my orders, ma'am."

"All right, fine. Where is he staying? I'll follow."

"Men only—"

"Men only, my eye," Mrs. Clyde burst out. "Now I understand why a handsome young fella like him can't come inside with these young women, but I'm old enough to be his ma, and I'm going to follow to his quarters, where I intend to take a look at his feet. Is that understood?"

"I'll try to get it approved, ma'am," the soldier said, his face red as he swallowed hard.

"You do that. Either way, I'm looking after this young man." She glared a "try to stop me" look at him, then turned to Grace. "Are you going to be all right, or do you need some looking after, too?"

Grace smiled at her with an affection she never thought herself possible of feeling for the dowager who, until this journey, Grace had only known as an overbearing suffragette fighter.

The soldier had deposited her trunk and carpetbag inside the cabin, so there was nothing to do but go inside and let Paul go to his own quarters. Grace met his gaze. "Thank you again, Mr. Spencer. I owe you my life."

As though no one else existed, he took her hand and lifted it to his lips. "I'll be around to speak with you later. And you know why."

Heat rose to her cheeks, but Mrs. Clyde spared her a reaction. "No, he won't. He'll be off those feet. Look at him: He can barely walk." She turned to Grace. "Get inside and warm yourself. I'll tend Mr. Spencer and will return as soon as possible."

The trio moved away as Melissa and Grace watched them go. Silently, the two women turned and entered the cabin. As soon as the door was closed and the leather latch connected, Melissa swung on her. "Exactly what went on between you two after Paul found you until now?"

twelve

The pain was unlike anything Paul had ever experienced, though Mrs. Clyde assured him pain was a good sign. It meant his hands and feet were getting blood flow instead of being blocks of dead nerves, bone, and skin. Paul wasn't sure which he preferred at the moment with his feet plunged into warm water. It was all he could do not to scream in agony. But he knew the alternative would be a loss of fingers or toes. So for the moment, he tried to be grateful for the pain.

Mrs. Clyde had soaked strips of flannel in warm water and had wrapped his hands, so they weren't feeling much better than his feet. She poured him a cup of coffee and turned to him with frank perusal. "You're going to have to marry her, you know."

Palming the tin cup between his two flannelled hands, Paul gave a short laugh. "I would have married her the first week of the journey."

"Is she aware of that?"

Nodding, Paul enjoyed the warm sensation in his throat as the coffee slid down. "I asked for her hand with rain soaking into my clothes. I had a sore throat for a week. I'm surprised I didn't catch pneumonia. Trust me, she knows how I feel."

The older woman added hot water to the basin. Paul groaned.

She scowled, shaking her head, and spoke as though she hadn't just set his feet, once again, on fire. "I vow, I've never met a more choosy old maid. She turned the reverend down, too."

Paul gripped the mug, but he didn't comment on the new information. Did Grace have feelings for the reverend? Was

121

that the reason she spent so much time with him?

"She's turned me down twice. Once in the rain, and once during a blizzard."

Mrs. Clyde frowned. "You mean to tell me Grace doesn't plan to marry you after spending an entire night alone with you?"

Paul fought to keep from spitting the most recent sip of coffee across the room. The woman's candor was nothing short of embarrassing. "That's pretty much what she said."

"Well, she'll just have to change her mind, and that's all there is to it. That young woman doesn't need to live with the stigma of compromise hanging over her head. Even if the circumstances were unavoidable, you know what people will surmise."

Paul nodded grimly, wishing she'd stop pushing his feet back into the water every time he lifted them out for a little relief.

"Stop being childish," she snapped. "I know it hurts, but this is the best way to get some real warmth back to your feet. Would you have preferred a block of ice that had to be removed completely?"

"Of course not." To say the least.

When Jonas came in two hours later, Mrs. Clyde had just finished bandaging Paul's feet and hands. She gave him a dose of laudanum and saw him tucked into bed. Paul allowed the pampering, but closed his eyes against Jonas's mocking grin.

She glanced at Jonas. "Change the bandages every three hours. His feet are raw and bleeding. But he'll keep all his toes. He should stay in bed except to get up and soak his feet in the salt water solution at least three times a day."

Jonas looked as though he wasn't sure what hit him, but he agreed.

Mrs. Clyde slipped on her coat and wrapped her scarf

securely around her neck. "Is Matilda in your cabin, Mrs. Clyde?" Jonas asked.

"She is. Why do you want to know?"

"Will you give her a note from me?"

She buttoned three large buttons up her torso. "Her pa still giving the two of you trouble?"

He nodded. "I'm not allowed near her, or Mr. Sands takes it out on Matilda."

"Well, I'm not one who normally approves of a child going against her pa's wishes, but Matilda's not exactly a child anymore." She opened her palm. "Give it here."

Jonas's face broke into a grin. "Thank you, ma'am. I'm obliged."

Tucking the letter into her coat pocket, she waved away his thanks. "Just take care of Mr. Spencer there. He's a stubborn one. And he doesn't want to soak his feet. But see that he does it anyway."

"Yes, ma'am."

Paul had a feeling Mrs. Clyde had just made a loyal friend for life. A loyalty that most likely meant Jonas would follow the dowager's instructions to the letter. For now, that wouldn't be such a bad thing—staying in bed, warm against the chill.

The wind was starting to howl again by the time Mrs. Clyde opened the door. "Looks like we're in for more weather," she said as she stepped outside.

"I'd walk you back to your quarters," Jonas said, "but Mr. Sands said I best not get anywhere near the cabin or else. He was mad they wouldn't give him and Tilly a cabin of their own like they gave the married couples. Said they were as much family as any of those other folks."

"I'll be just fine," Mrs. Clyde assured him. "It's not far, and the snow isn't coming down that hard yet."

Jonas watched her from outside their door until Mrs. Clyde was close to her cabin; then he stepped back in and headed straight for the fire.

The laudanum was beginning to affect Paul. Warmth flooded his body, and heavy rocks seemed to sit on his eyelids. What he wouldn't give to surrender. He forced himself to stay awake long enough to say, "I thought you had decided not to court Miss Sands since her pa is so dead set against the notion."

Jonas blew into his hands, then spread them palms down above the fire. "I couldn't let her go." A humorless burst of laughter escaped him. "This must be God's way of having a fine joke at my expense. His way of acquiring restitution for the hearts I've broken along the way." He drew a breath and turned. "We have to find a way to be together."

"Just be careful."

"We are." Jonas turned. "What happened between you and Miss Porter? I was at the Bullocks' a few minutes ago and Mrs. Bullock was saying it wasn't decent that you two spent the night in the same wagon."

Word certainly spread fast through the members of the wagon train. "How do they know?"

"It's true then?"

"It's true that we were forced to occupy the same space for the night after I found her in the blizzard. But of course, everything was innocent."

"I would never have thought otherwise."

"You didn't tell me—how did you hear about it?"

"The soldiers have been taking ox meat from cabin to cabin, and one of them explained the situation to folks. Apparently, everyone is aware of it by now. I reckon we'll all be attending a wedding before long?"

Paul's tongue felt thick in his mouth, and his chest rose and fell in a heavy breath. He couldn't fight sleep much longer. "I will if she'll stop being stubborn and say yes."

Jonas's eyebrows rose. "Why would she turn you down?"

"She'd rather be compromised than take a chance on loving the children." He felt himself drifting. "I don't know why, though. I really don't." From a distance he heard Jonas speaking but couldn't make any sense of his friend's words.

Unable to fight sleep's pull any longer, he surrendered. Tomorrow would take care of itself, as the Bible said. For now, he'd concentrate on getting better so he could find a way to change Grace's mind.

Just before darkness claimed him, he heard the wind scream. Another blizzard. For the life of him, he wished he was shivering in a wagon on the plains with Grace rather than here in a warm bed without her.

≈

The warmth of the fire did little to warm the mood in the cabin. Of the two cabins allotted for single females, Grace found herself unfortunate enough to share with Melissa.

"I'd never stoop to getting myself caught in a blizzard just to get a man's attention." Melissa directed her comments at Grace as she sashayed across the dusty room. She glanced back over her shoulder. "I suppose you'll expect a proposal now."

"Really, Melissa," Mrs. Clyde broke in. "That's enough of this silliness."

Melissa ignored the interruption. "Don't count on marrying him. Paul loves me. I don't think he'll give me up that easily just because an old maid like you was silly enough to get yourself compromised."

Old maid? Grace met Melissa's venomous glare. Oh what she wouldn't give to put this haughty, presumptive woman in her place. To say that Paul had proposed to her already, not once, but twice, and wasn't it odd that he should do so when his heart beat for Melissa alone?

But she wouldn't shame her mama's memory with such rudeness, of course. If not for the bounds of propriety. . .

For that reason alone, she didn't mention Paul's proposal.

That would make matters much worse, and since they had to share quarters for the next several months, it would be better to try to keep the peace as much as possible.

"I'm sorry you feel that way, Melissa."

"Are you?" Her disdainful tone set Grace's teeth on edge, and she couldn't resist a little defense of herself. After all, there was no one else to defend her, was there?

"I am sorry that anyone could be foolish enough to believe I deliberately got caught alone during a blizzard. As though I would risk my life on the very slight chance that Mr. Spencer might come back for me." She shook her head. "Really, Melissa. Use a little common sense."

Melissa's eyes narrowed to mere slits. "Are you mocking me, Grace?"

Valerie gave a little gasp. "Please, Melissa, don't quarrel."

Melissa glared at Valerie, who sat on her bed, staring at her hands.

"Mind your own business, little sister."

Mrs. Clyde rattled a few pans next to the stove and pulled out a large pot. "I don't see how Grace could keep from it, my girl. Only an idiot would get deliberately caught in a storm for the sake of a man. Besides, I happen to know that Paul. . ."

"Would have gone into a storm for anyone," Grace finished, sending Mrs. Clyde a definite glance of warning.

"My uncle wouldn't marry you anyway, Melissa."

"Bobbin," Grace admonished, "please use your manners when you speak with an adult. You will address Miss Turner properly. Understood?"

"Well, he wouldn't marry Miss Turner." Bobbin sneered, raising her chin. "He knows the boys and me don't want her for our new ma."

Melissa's mouth dropped open. "You don't?" Hers was a look of one who has only just realized the world didn't adore her unconditionally. Grace almost felt sorry for her. Until her next words. She waved away Bobbin's observation. "Well, what do you all know? You're nothing but spoiled, unruly children. Something I intend to remedy as soon as I am your uncle's wife."

Bobbin folded her arms across her chest. "I'll run off and live with the Indians."

Melissa met her glare for glare and folded her own arms. The standoff reminded Grace of two willful children. "Good. Take your brothers with you. That will save me the trouble of convincing your uncle to send you to an orphanage where you belong."

"Uncle Paul would never do that!" Fury sparked from Bobbin's eyes. "You. . .you. . ."

"It's all right, child." Mrs. Clyde set a bowl of potatoes and a knife in front of Bobbin. "Put all that energy into peeling these for our supper. My roast will melt in your mouth," she said, none too modestly. "I'm sorry you lost your ox, Grace, but I'm mighty glad to get some fresh meat in my belly."

Why the soldiers didn't put Paul and the children into a cabin of their own, Grace couldn't for the life of her imagine. According to Mrs. Clyde, Paul's boys would be moving in with Paul and Jonas as soon as he healed up a little better. For now, they were bunking with the soldiers. Elmer was enraptured with the chance to be so near the blue-uniformed men.

But Bobbin wasn't thrilled. That afternoon, Tilly and Valerie had made up little games to keep the child occupied. Melissa's open animosity toward both Bobbin and Grace made things uncomfortable. Grace observed the older woman as she went about preparing for the meal. There was no denying Mrs. Clyde had lost a considerable amount of weight since the journey began. A new vitality had come over her, and she smiled more. She seemed to have lost her hard edge, that defensive attitude that Grace supposed came along with being a pioneer of something as important and volatile as the idea that women should be allowed to vote.

Mrs. Clyde slipped a note to Matilda. The girl's face brightened. She settled onto her bed and opened the paper.

"Well?" Melissa's haughty tone reverberated through the cabin. "Who is it from?"

Matilda's shy face turned a deep red. "I. . .I can't really—"

"Oh for mercy's sake," Melissa said, dropping onto her bunk. "Don't tell us then." She rolled her eyes and flopped onto her stomach, resting her head on the pillow she hugged.

Mrs. Clyde planted her hands on her hips and cocked an eyebrow toward Melissa. "Don't get too comfortable. We have chores to do."

It was almost funny the way Melissa's eyes widened in horror at the suggestion. "What chores?"

"Someone has to wash and dry dishes. The room hasn't had a good cleaning in ages, from what I can tell. So take your pick. Sweep and scrub the floor, or start on dishes."

"I don't know why you are the one to dole out the chores."

Mrs. Clyde's narrow-eyed gaze cut a line across the room between them. But Melissa didn't back down. She raised herself up on one elbow and returned the glare.

Bobbin struggled to her feet. She had mastered the use of her crutches and seemed to be getting much better. Maneuvering to the wash basin, she lifted the first dish. With her leg bent at the knee, she looked as though she might fall if not for the support of the counter and crutches. "I'll do dishes, ma'am."

Pride wrapped itself around Grace's heart. She figured the little girl was only doing it to spite Melissa and make the girl appear even more self-centered than she already looked. Nonetheless, it showed grit. And that was always impressive.

Mrs. Clyde had apparently come to the same conclusion. She grinned and winked at Bobbin. "Can you stand that long and use both hands? What about balancing?"

"I can lean against the cabinet as long as I keep my leg up like this."

Melissa smiled broadly. "Well, then. I guess I'm not needed after all."

Mrs. Clyde appeared to have reached her limit of good spirits, and a bit of the woman Grace had known back in Missouri emerged. She shot across the dusty floor, broom in hand. Grace feared she might be planning to attack. Apparently, so did Melissa, for she shoved up from the bed and stood, ready to defend herself if necessary. Not that she would have been any match for the dowager.

"Now you take this broom and get yourself to work sweeping the floor. If that little girl can do her fair share when she only has one leg to stand on, you can surely get your little behind to work."

Melissa's cheeks glowed a shiny red. She rolled her eyes. "I'm not very good at chores. I don't like doing them." She turned toward Valerie. "My sister will do mine and hers."

Mrs. Clyde's lips turned white and her voice lowered. "No, little miss, she will not. If you don't work, you won't eat."

"But I told you, I am no good. I'll just be a burden to you all."

"That's fine. If you don't do it right the first time, at least we don't have anywhere to go. You will have plenty of time to keep trying until you get it clean."

Matilda, Bobbin, Valerie, and Grace watched the exchange in silence. No one wanted to be on the receiving end of either of these women's sharp tongues. Better to let them fight it out between themselves.

Realizing Mrs. Clyde had years of stubbornness more than she did, Melissa gave in with a customary huff. She snatched the broom away and attacked the floor, raising the dust until it swirled through the air like a small twister.

Grace's nose tickled, Matilda sneezed, and Mrs. Clyde pretended she didn't notice a thing. But Grace could tell by the way she cleared her throat and wrinkled her nose that the dust was disturbing her as well. As it turned out, Melissa did a fine job. With one silky eyebrow raised and an expression that could only be described as haughty, she handed the broom back to Mrs. Clyde.

"There, you see? You did that just like you've been doing it all of your life."

Melissa jerked her chin and turned back to her bunk.

"What are you doing?" Mrs. Clyde asked.

"I'm going to rest on my bunk. I did my chore."

"What about washing the floor?"

Grace had to fight the urge to ask the two women to stop their bickering.

"Do you honestly expect me to do all the filthy work around here?"

Grace stared back at her from the window she was scrubbing. The dirt was an inch thick, and even scrubbing until her arms ached hadn't removed more than the first layer. She was tempted to shove the rag in the selfish woman's face and show her just what dirty work was.

Tilly stared at her from washing down the dirty log walls and wordlessly shook her head. But she gathered a breath. "I'll do the floors."

"Wonderful!" Melissa dimpled and she turned the first approving look on Matilda that Grace had ever observed. "You're so sweet. It's a shame your father won't allow Jonas near you. He used to think so highly of you."

Did the girl even think about how her words might feel? No. She couldn't possibly. No one could be that blatantly hurtful to a person as kind and unassuming as Matilda.

"Who, may I ask, are you staring at?"

Grace met Melissa's venomous glare. "I couldn't help but wonder if you know how unkind you are."

All color drained from Melissa's face. Her jaw dropped,

and for the first time since Grace had known the girl, it appeared as though she had lost the ability to brandish her weapon. Her silence gave Grace the opening to continue.

"Perhaps you've never experienced the blessing of having a friend or someone in authority to teach you how to treat folks. But your remarks toward Tilly are cruel."

Tilly gave up being the good soldier, and her face crumpled. She dropped to the wooden chair nearest her, bent at the waist, and pressed her face into the palms of her hands.

"Now, look what you've done," Melissa cried. "And you said I was cruel. She was just fine until you started accusing me."

Mrs. Clyde moved across the room, tossing out a frustrated breath as she walked by Melissa. She grabbed another chair. It scraped across the floor and joined the mournful sound of Tilly's soft weeping.

Mrs. Clyde stared above Tilly's head, nearly knocking Melissa over with the sheer force of her disdain. Melissa sucked in a sharp breath. Her skirt swished as she spun around and flounced to her bed. She lay on her side with her back to the room.

It appeared the young woman had nothing more to say.

Bobbin took in the entire scene from her place at the counter, where she had just finished washing the last pot. Her arms trembled, and Grace feared her shoulders might not support her weight as she maneuvered the crutches across the room. She walked over to the little girl. "May I help you?" she whispered.

Bobbin stared up at her and nodded. "My underarms hurt."

"Don't fret. Give me the crutches, and I'll set them against the chair and carry you to your bunk. Which one is it?"

"I don't have one, Miss Porter."

Grace looked around. The child was right. There were five bunks, apparently for the adults. "You may sit on my bed for now. We'll discuss the particulars of your sleeping arrangements later."

"She can sleep with me, Miss Porter," Valerie said. "We're both pretty small. I'll sleep at one end, and she at the other."

Bobbin grinned. "Thank you." She looked at Grace. "Can I still sit on your bed?"

"I suppose so. For a little while."

Bobbin gave up her crutches. Grace kept the girl steady with one arm while setting the crutches aside with the other. Then she lifted the girl, surprising herself with how much stronger she'd become since beginning the journey. She smiled at the thought. What would Ralph think of her now? Certainly he never would have believed she could hitch and unhitch her own oxen, cook over an open fire, and survive a blizzard.

Once Grace settled Bobbin on her bed, she was able to turn her attention back to Mrs. Clyde and Tilly. Mrs. Clyde offered a hankie, and the young woman blew her nose. "I know I should be grateful for all the things God's given me," she said around a gulp of air. "But I can't help but wish He'd give me Jonas, too."

Melissa harrumphed.

"Well, honey," Mrs. Clyde said, ignoring Melissa entirely. "Perhaps God has shown you that Jonas is the one for you. Often the gifts God chooses to give are met with opposition."

Tilly cut Mrs. Clyde a glance. "Do you think so?"

"Well, I'm not the Lord, nor am I a prophet, but I believe the answer will work itself out."

Melissa turned. "I don't see how you can be so selfish."

Grace fought to keep from laughing aloud at the pot calling the kettle black. Mrs. Clyde, however, wasn't as self-controlled.

"What's so funny?" Melissa demanded.

"You—calling anyone else in this room selfish."

"Well, she is. She knows what her pa would do to Jonas if he found out she's in love with him." She nibbled her lip. "Don't you care what happens to him?"

"Of course I do." Tilly's voice barely rose above a whisper. "I would never want Jonas to be harmed. I've tried to break it off with him. But he's. . .persistent."

Melissa's face softened, and she seemed to grow a heart for a second. "My brother is strong-willed." She smiled. "Ma always said he would be the death of her." Her face clouded. "He wasn't of course. She died in childbirth."

Grace's heart went out to her again. "I'm sorry, Melissa. I know how difficult it is to lose your mother. Mine died when I was fourteen."

"Then it isn't exactly the same thing, is it?" Melissa retorted. "I was only two."

"Why did your pa never remarry?" Tilly asked.

"Because he was devoted to his children."

"Just like Uncle Paul is devoted to us."

Melissa gave a huff, but thankfully she let the fight go.

Mrs. Clyde glanced at Grace as she addressed the little girl. "Your uncle Paul will marry, but only when it's the right woman who will love you, too."

thirteen

Paul awoke to the aroma of frying bacon and the sound of whispering. He opened his eyes and sat up, resting on his elbow. Lester stood over the stove. "Hey, Les," he said. "Where's Jonas?"

Lester turned. He shrugged. "I haven't seen him. You want coffee?"

"Yeah, but I can get it."

"No, sir," Elmer said. "Last night, Mr. Jonas said you have to stay off your feet until Mrs. Clyde says otherwise." He got up from the table, poured a cup, and walked carefully and almost painfully slowly across the room. "Here ya go, Uncle Paul."

Paul couldn't help the smile that curved his lips as his heart filled with love for the little guy. He ruffled the five-year-old's hair. "Thanks, pal."

The door opened letting in icy air. Bear stepped in, carrying an armload of wood. "Whew it's really cold out there."

"Is it still snowing?" Lester asked.

"Yeah, but there's no wind."

Paul sipped his coffee. "I wonder where Jonas went so early."

Bear dropped the wood by the stove and turned, slapping his hands together. "He left last night."

"He did?"

"Yes, sir."

Alarm seized him. "In the blizzard?"

Bear nodded. "I tried to stop him, but he said he had to do something."

"He didn't say what?"

"No, sir. But he said he'd be back today or tomorrow."

"That's it?"

Two raps on the door drew their attention away from the conversation. Elmer let Mrs. Clyde in. Paul sucked in a breath at the sight of her. His feet burned like fire just thinking about what she was about to do to them. She pulled the scarf from her face and glanced around the room. "Jonas isn't here?"

"We were just discussing it," Paul said. "Bear saw him leave in the night."

Worry creased her brow.

Her obvious concern lent fire to Paul's own worry. "Mrs. Clyde? Is something wrong?"

"Tilly's missing, too."

Swinging his legs around to the side of the bed, Paul sat up. "I have to go find them before Sands figures out she's gone."

"Don't you dare think you're going anywhere, my boy. Jonas is a grown man. He knew the risk."

"He left in a blizzard."

"Yes, and so did you a couple of days ago."

The boys grinned, and Elmer giggled at the reminder.

Paul scowled. "That was different."

Mrs. Clyde nodded. "I'll have to agree with you there. But I'm afraid you might have given Jonas the idea."

"You mean they deliberately got caught in a blizzard overnight so there would be no choice but to let them get married?"

"That's my thinking. Do you think they'd be foolish enough to go through with something like that?"

Paul didn't think. He knew. Jonas wasn't above a little duplicity to get what he wanted, and if he wanted Matilda Sands, he would do anything to get her. He wouldn't let a little thing like a disapproving father stand in his way.

"I have to go after him, Mrs. Clyde. If I don't, and Sands does, Jonas could likely be killed."

"Do you want to lose your feet?" She grabbed a pot from the stove. Turning to Bear, she handed him the pot. "Please go out and fill this as over full as possible with snow so I can warm it for your uncle's soak."

"Yes, ma'am." Still in his coat, Bear took the pot and headed across the room.

"How's Bobbin?" Paul asked.

"Feisty as ever." She smiled. "Don't worry. We're taking good care of her. Especially Miss Porter."

Paul couldn't resist a smile.

Mrs. Clyde chortled. "I thought you'd like hearing that."

"You think she's coming around?"

"Could be. She still holds the child aloof other than making sure she's safe and fed. But she's fond of Bobbin, even if she does try to resist."

"Do you know what happened?" Paul hesitated, trying to figure out exactly what he wanted to ask. "She seems fragile when it comes to getting close to anyone, especially children. I can't help but wonder why she goes against all of her natural instincts—marriage, children. Especially when it's so obvious that she'd like to accept my proposal."

"Oh, you think so?" She seemed amused, which sent a flash of heat up the back of his neck. But he knew what he knew. Or at least what he thought he knew.

Still shaking her head, Mrs. Clyde unbuttoned her coat. Elmer was at her side in a flash. "I will help you, ma'am," he said. The old woman melted like an icicle in a pot of water. "Why, thank you, young man." She cupped his chin. "Who taught you to be such a gentleman?"

Elmer stared up at her with wide, earnest eyes. "My ma."

He carefully arranged her coat across his arms so that it wouldn't drag on the floor and walked to his bunk, where he took great care to lay it across the covers. "It'll be safe there," he announced, giving the wool garment a pat.

Mrs. Clyde nodded, remaining serious, though her eyes danced. "Thank you, again."

Lester slid the bacon onto a plate. "Mrs. Clyde, have you had breakfast, ma'am?"

"An hour ago. Miss Porter cooked, and the dishes are already wiped clean."

Paul asked, "What is Miss Porter doing today?"

"I believe she intends to send a telegram to her brother." Mrs. Clyde frowned as though remembering. "After that, I believe she intends to discuss the subject of Christmas with a few of the fort's women. It's right around the corner, you know."

"Christmas?" Elmer's face lit.

"That's right." An indulgent smile tipped Mrs. Clyde's lips. "What do you like best about the holiday?"

A tiny frown creased his brow as he tried to focus on an answer. Finally, he took a deep breath. "Ma always gave me an orange and a peppermint stick. Last year, I got a new shirt."

Paul stared at the little boy, and the icy blast that hit him had little to do with the door opening as Bear returned. For the first time since his sister had died, he realized something: The children had grown out of their clothes. The thought that they knew and hadn't wanted to mention their need smashed at his core. What would Carrie think of the way he had neglected that basic need?

"Don't look so downcast, my boy," Mrs. Clyde said as she set the pot on the stove. She carried a handful of flannel bandages to his bunk. "Hands first," she said. She lowered her voice. "Now that you see they need clothes, you can do something about it."

"I have to go find something for them to wear."

Pain seared through his hands as Mrs. Clyde began to pull

the bandages away from his fingers. He sucked in a breath to keep from groaning.

"Sore, are they?"

"Yes."

"Imagine what your feet will be like." She looked over her shoulder. "How's that water doing?"

"It's warm, Mrs. Clyde."

"Good." She left him and went to the stove, filled a washbowl with the water, and brought it back. "Let's clean those hands. Do you need some laudanum first?"

He shook his head. If he hadn't slept so deeply the night before, he'd have been awake when Jonas had left, maybe even have talked him out of it.

Thirty minutes later, after the excruciating pain of removing bandages and soaking his feet was past, Mrs. Clyde tossed the old bandages into the fire and cleaned the bowl and pot. Paul's jaw clenched and unclenched. He fought to keep from crying out. Fifteen minutes after she finished, his feet still screamed.

Mrs. Clyde helped him lie down. "Now, do you still think you should go after Jonas or wander outside looking for new clothes for the children?"

Scowling, he shook his head. "I reckon not."

A knock at the door startled him. Bear left the table, where he was just finishing up breakfast. "Paul!" came the panicked sound of Grace's cry. She stood shaking on the threshold as Bear opened the door.

"What's wrong?" Paul sat up, tried to stand, but his feet wouldn't support him. He dropped back onto his bed, clenching his jaw.

Grace stared at him. "You're all bandaged up. Your feet and hands?" She turned her gaze on Mrs. Clyde, her eyebrows raised.

"He was this close to frostbite. He should thank the

Almighty on bended knee."

"I had no idea you were so bad off, Mr. Spencer." The compassion in her eyes was worth the pain, as far as Paul was concerned. It proved that she felt something for him. Maybe not enough to accept his proposal, but definitely, her feelings were headed in the right direction.

Mrs. Clyde gave a shrug. "I thought it best not to tell you the extent of his injuries."

"But why?"

"No sense in you feeling guilty. You know how you take everything to heart."

"I'm so sorry, Paul. I had no idea," she said again.

"It's not your fault." He smiled, hoping to convince her that he truly didn't blame her.

"But if I had just stayed with the wagon train, you wouldn't be in this situation."

Mrs. Clyde planted her hands on her hips. "This is ridiculous. What happened out there that sent you running to Mr. Spencer in the first place?"

Grace's face flushed a beguiling pink. "I. . .well, I didn't come running to him."

But she had, and that act spoke volumes to Paul's heart. "What's wrong, Grace?"

Without stumbling over his use of her first name, Grace took a deep breath. "Mr. Sands is looking for Tilly. She's gone. He said he's going to get the captain of the fort and come here looking for Jonas. He suspects they might have run off. Is he here?"

Paul shook his head. "We were just coming to the same conclusion. I hate to think poorly of my friend, but I figure they might have purposely run away so they will be forced to get married."

"That foolish girl." Grace sat hard on one of the wooden chairs. "Why do such a thing?"

"My guess is that she loved him enough to risk her reputation. Not to mention her pa's wrath."

There was no time for more speculation. Mr. Sands burst into the cabin, letting in a blast of cold. "Where is he?"

A soldier walked in behind him. Definitely not the captain. Paul looked closer and recognized sergeant stripes. The soldier removed his cap. "I apologize for the intrusion."

"What seems to be the trouble?" Paul asked, determined to give nothing away.

The vein on Mr. Sands's neck stood out, pumping hard, and Paul wondered if the man should lie down a moment and gather his composure. Mr. Sands narrowed his eyes and shot sparks of anger in Paul's direction. "Don't pretend you don't know who we're after."

The sergeant held up his hand to silence the irate father. "Is Jonas Turner here?"

"No, he isn't," Paul said.

"When was the last time you saw him?"

"I'm not sure. Before supper last night. I fell asleep early."

Mrs. Clyde motioned to his feet and hands. "Mr. Spencer is recovering from frostbite. I gave him a heavy dose of laudanum last night. It's no wonder he slept so soundly."

Mr. Sands turned to the sergeant. "I want a search party organized immediately. It's apparent my daughter was captured and taken against her will."

"I highly doubt that," Mrs. Clyde said. "I am almost positive she would have gone anywhere with Mr. Turner. He wouldn't have had to force her."

"Are you suggesting my daughter is a loose woman? Wanton?" Mr. Sands's eyes bulged, his face mottled with anger.

"Of course she isn't suggesting any such thing," Grace said, her face flushed at the very thought. "Tilly is a lovely girl. A good girl. Mrs. Clyde and I share a cabin with her. We're both quite taken with her."

The sergeant looked from one woman to the other. "Are you so close to her that you'd help her sneak away?"

"I'm telling you, my Tilly wouldn't sneak off. If she's with him, you can take my word for it he took her against her will."

Mrs. Clyde shoved her hands onto her hips. "We seem to have differing opinions on that matter, Mr. Sands."

"Well, what do you expect from those two?" His hands swept the air between Grace and Paul.

"Now hang on a second, Mr. Sands," Paul broke in, but it didn't do much to shut the man's mouth.

"These two spent the night together in a blizzard. I reckon they'll be getting themselves married off soon." The words no sooner left his mouth than Mr. Sands grew pale. His voice shook. "I'll kill him," he said in a hoarse whisper.

The sergeant sent him a look of caution. "Be careful, sir. You don't want to say anything that might point to you if Mr. Turner ends up dead."

"But don't you see that Mr. Spencer put his friend up to the same nonsense? It's too much to be coincidence that these two were caught together in a blizzard and now Mr. Turner has done the same thing to my daughter."

Grace squared her shoulders, her lips white, hands shaking. "First of all, Mr. Sands. Mr. Spencer didn't do anything to me. I was stuck in a storm, and he came to find me. I might have died without his bravery. And look, his hands and feet are wounded because of me." Her voice broke ever so slightly.

The gentle force of her words smashed all of Paul's defenses, what few he had left where she was concerned. He found himself lifting a silent prayer that she would *please* marry him.

Grace continued with eloquence, her voice calm. "Mr. Sands, I don't know the circumstances of Tilly and Jonas's disappearance, but I can almost assure you without doubt that your daughter is very much in love with Jonas. And the feelings are reciprocated. I feel sure that if they are indeed together, she went willingly."

The sergeant scratched at his jaw. "All right. I'll put together a small search party, and we'll scout the area. The snow didn't let up until early in the morning hours, so I don't expect there will be much in the way of tracks, but we'll do our best."

Mr. Sands stomped to the door. "I'm coming with you." He turned and shoved a finger toward Paul. "You'd best hope nothing's happened to my little girl."

Paul matched his glare. "I don't take kindly to threats, sir."

"Let's go." The sergeant opened the door and practically shoved Mr. Sands over the threshold. He turned back to Paul. "Heaven forbid anything happened to that girl. You'd best be on your guard."

Sober caution settled over Paul, especially now when he could barely hobble. He doubted he could even hold a gun. How would he protect his family if Mr. Sands got it into his head that Paul was responsible for Tilly's absence?

He felt Grace's focus on him. Slowly, he raised his gaze to meet hers. Self-condemnation clouded her face, from her eyes to her lips, which were pressed together as she breathed sharply through her nose. She stared at his wrapped hands, his wrapped feet. "It's okay, Grace. They look worse than they are. If you hadn't spent hours rubbing the blood back into them, I would have lost my toes and probably my fingers, too. Please don't blame yourself."

Averting her gaze, she ran her tongue over her lips. "I should get back to the cabin. I hate to leave Melissa alone with Bobbin. They tend to upset each other." Her eyes widened. "Although I'm sure they could learn to get along if. . ."

Paul frowned. If what?

It wasn't until she slipped from the cabin that he realized

she meant that if he married Melissa, the two would learn to get along.

Somehow he had to convince the stubborn love of his life that he wouldn't give up. He'd pursue her relentlessly until she gave in.

fourteen

Grace didn't stop until she reached the door of her cabin. Out of breath and cheeks burning despite the frigid air, she reached forward just as a commotion toward the gate drew her thoughts away from her own desperate guilt.

A lone horse rode through, carrying two people. A female in front, a male behind her. Only a fool couldn't have guessed who those two riders were.

Though she knew it was none of her affair, Grace couldn't resist the pull toward the gate. She backtracked, meeting Mrs. Clyde, who was just leaving Paul's cabin.

"It looks as though Jonas and Tilly have come back."

Mrs. Clyde gave a sharp nod and gathered in a breath. "Looks that way."

Mr. Sands stomped toward them and reached up. He snatched his daughter by her wrist and would have yanked her from the horse if Jonas hadn't interfered. He tightened his grip around her waist. "Leave her alone, Mr. Sands." Jonas's voice held a quiet warning.

"Boy, you'd best turn my daughter loose. I aim to punish her properly. And if you think this means you're going to marry her, you can forget it!"

"Mr. Sands, I've already married Tilly." Jonas's eyes glittered as cold as ice. "She's my wife, and I won't let you hurt her ever again."

"It's a lie! It's a lie!" Horror widened the man's eyes. "Gal, you'd best get down from there."

"It's true, Pa." Tilly's voice shook. "Jonas and I were married before we left the camp."

Reverend Ellis elbowed through the curious onlookers. "It's true. These two came to me last evening, and I pronounced them man and wife."

"Ridiculous!" Mr. Sands sputtered. "This man isn't a real reverend."

Reverend Ellis drew himself up tall, obviously offended by the very accusation. "I have documentation to prove that I am indeed a reverend in God's eyes as well as the eyes of my church."

The sergeant stepped forward. "Mr. Sands, it appears your daughter has been legally married according to the laws of the land. At the risk of being indelicate in the presence of ladies, may I point out that these two have been alone all night. It seems as though it would be in your daughter's best interests for you to step back and accept that she has acted outside of your authority and is now a married woman. Lawfully, you have no more rights to her. And this fort stands behind the marriage."

Grace tensed as Mr. Sands clenched and unclenched his fists.

Only once had she seen anger such as this in a man's face. She tried to close her mind against the image of Sammie's broken body, but it did no good.

Mr. Sands shoved a shaky finger toward Tilly. "You're no daughter of mine. You hear?"

Tears rolled down Tilly's face as she nodded.

Mr. Sands spun on his boots. His eyes, filled with hate, rested on Grace. He launched forward. Grace gasped, stepping back.

He kept up the advance, hurling accusations. "This is your fault. Yours and that man of yours."

Mrs. Clyde stepped between Grace and the irate man. She brandished a palm-sized revolver. "You'd best stop right there, Mister, or I'll plug you. You hear? This might be a small weapon, but it'll get the job done."

The cold steel in her voice alarmed Grace, but she could have wept with relief as Mr. Sands stopped dead in his tracks, eyeing the weapon. "This ain't over," he hissed.

But Mrs. Clyde was having none of his thinly veiled threats. "It better be if you know what's good for you. This young lady didn't have anything to do with your daughter's secret marriage. If you'd like to look for someone to blame, go look in a mirror. What's happened with Jonas and Tilly is your own fault. A girl can only take so much being knocked around. I'm surprised she stayed loyal to you this long."

His cheeks puffed out, but he didn't respond. The sergeant strode toward him. "Are we going to have any trouble out of you, Mr. Sands?"

A moment of tense silence thickened the air. Grace held her breath. Finally, Mr. Sands seemed to cap his rage enough to gain control. "No, sir. Not from me."

"Good."

With one more venomous glare, Mr. Sands stalked away.

Sergeant Rawlings lifted both of his hands. "All right, folks. There's nothing more to see here. Let's break it up and give the newlyweds some room to breathe."

Jonas climbed down and reached up for his bride. One look at her radiant face, and no one could doubt whatsoever that Tilly was a delirious, happy bride.

A brush of skirts whooshed by Grace, and she nearly slipped on the icy ground. Melissa strode forward. "What is this?" She stared from one to the other. "What have you done, Jonas?"

"I've given you another sister."

"What?" She glanced from Jonas to Tilly, her eyes registering the truth. "Are you out of your mind? I saw Mr. Sands when I came out of the cabin. He told me he was going to set this right."

A chill passed over Grace. But Jonas didn't seem affected. Likely his brain was too swelled with love and happiness to consider the danger he and Tilly might truly be in from her pa. Mr. Sands didn't seem to be the sort of man to forgive and surrender very easily.

Leaning, Jonas pressed a kiss to Melissa's cheek. "Be happy for me."

Melissa sniffed. "I don't think that's likely to happen. You've not only married a girl who isn't nearly good enough for you, but one selfish enough to put you in danger."

Grace had had enough of the young woman's poison. Stepping forward, she grabbed Melissa's arm. "Let's go."

Melissa jerked her arm away. "I'll go on my own. I've decided to visit Paul. At least he understands me."

As Melissa strode away, jealousy twisted inside Grace, and she fought hard to push it away. After all, what right did she have? Paul would marry someone eventually. If not Melissa, then another woman. She had to let him go. As a matter of fact, she had something she needed to discuss with the sergeant. "Excuse me, Mrs. Clyde. I have to run an errand."

"You're just going to let that spoiled little hellion go after Paul? Without any sort of fight whatsoever?"

"It's none of my business."

"You're a foolish young woman, Grace. And a disappointment." Mrs. Clyde shook her head. "I have no idea why you're throwing away happiness like this. I can't even imagine it. But you know I'm a woman who speaks her mind, so let me just tell you: Paul Spencer loves you. He'd make a fine husband—a much better husband than that little floozy deserves."

Grace couldn't help but gasp. "Mrs. Clyde!"

"Perhaps she isn't exactly a floozy, but she's spoiled and mean-spirited, and if Paul marries her, not only will he be unhappy, but she will make those children miserable."

"Please, Mrs. Clyde. There's simply nothing I can do about the situation." Giving her heart to a child was the least of Grace's worries. The last thing she was going to do again was allow a child to trust her to keep him safe. Inevitably, she would fail, and Paul's children would be hurt.

The disappointment on Mrs. Clyde's face said it all. "Well, I have an appointment with the captain's wife. We're going to discuss a Christmas dinner celebration."

Grace nodded. "I'm on the committee to help decorate the cabin where we'll be eating, and they've enlisted me to help cook the meal. With Christmas only a week off, there's not much time to string beads and such, but we'll do our best. They already have decorations with baby Jesus in a manger and angels. Some of the soldiers worked together last winter to carve them out.

"There will be a large tree in one corner. The children will all get one gift, which the women of the fort have been making since this summer. They want to be sure the Indian children outside of the fort also receive something."

Grace imagined the look on Elmer's face when he opened a gift. The boy needed a new shirt. She'd noticed him eyeing Jonas's buckskins since the journey began. "Do you think the Indians would consider trading for a set of buckskins?"

"Probably. But why on earth would you want some?"

Grace shook her head. "Not for me."

Mrs. Clyde's mouth stretched wide into a grin. "Paul, then?"

"No." Grace let out a breath. "If you must know, I was thinking of Elmer. But that doesn't mean I'll actually get him some, though heaven knows he could use some clothes that fit."

"You've noticed?"

"Who wouldn't?"

Mrs. Clyde shrugged. "That's something a woman who

cares about a child might notice. I'd wager Melissa wouldn't know if he had on gold rings."

Grace scowled. "Gold rings on a child. Land's sakes, the very thought."

"You go ahead and pretend you don't know you're the woman that family needs. But I'm not fooled." Mrs. Clyde jerked her thumb in the direction of Paul's cabin. "That brazen girl is in there right now. If you were smart, you'd follow her and not let her sweet talk him into a tizzy."

"I'll do no such thing." If Paul was so easily manipulated, then he deserved what he got. The very idea! Grace whipped around, ready to head straight to her cabin.

"Wait, Grace." Mrs. Clyde slipped the revolver into her hand.

Grace opened her mouth to protest.

"No. You take it," Mrs. Clyde insisted. "Mr. Sands isn't bluffing. He's going to do something dangerous, and when he does, I want you protected since you and Paul seem to be the ones he blames most."

Hesitating only briefly, Grace nodded. "Thank you."

She fingered the weapon. She'd always had such an aversion to guns, to any sort of violence. But she couldn't help wondering if things might have been different that night if she had prevented Sammie's pa from taking him away from her.

fifteen

Paul wanted nothing more than to ask Melissa to please go away. She sat on the edge of his bed in a manner that made him uncomfortable. Bear's face was red, and Elmer and Lester gaped openmouthed as she tried to hold Paul's hand. Only the fact that both hands were wrapped gave him a polite excuse to ask her not to squeeze them.

"How did you get past the guard, Melissa? You know women aren't supposed to be in here. Even Mrs. Clyde has a hard time getting permission to nurse my hands and feet."

She flashed her alluring smile and gave a simple wave toward the door. "I promised the guard a waltz at the Christmas dance."

"That's all it took?" At Bear's incredulous tone, Paul swallowed a grin.

Melissa narrowed her gaze at the boy and scowled. "Of course." She turned wide eyes back to Paul.

"Oh, Paul, can you believe Jonas married that horrid girl?"

"I like Tilly," he replied, surprised Melissa could think ill of her. "She's been through a lot, but she and Jonas love each other. Your brother'll be happy. Maybe you should try to be happy for him."

Her eyes filled. "But Mr. Sands might go after Jonas. He's so angry."

"Your brother can take care of himself. And his new wife."

"If not for that horrid Miss Porter, they never would have done this."

Paul's gut knotted at her criticism of Grace. "Miss Porter

150

had nothing to do with this. How can you suggest such a thing?"

"Oh, Paul. Don't be angry. I couldn't bear to have you upset with me."

Paul's heart went out to her. "I'm not. I just don't feel comfortable discussing Miss Porter this way."

"But if she hadn't gotten herself lost on purpose, she wouldn't have put such an idea into Tilly's head. Jonas never would have married her otherwise."

"I hate to tell you, Melissa, but Jonas is the one determined to have Tilly even if it meant doing something drastic so that they had no choice but to marry. If anyone is to blame, it's your brother. You know how strong-willed he is. Do you honestly think that shy girl is that manipulative?"

She jerked her chin. "The quiet girls are the worst. They're the ones you most have to watch out for, Paul."

A disgusted snort across the room accompanied Elmer as he hopped up from the table where he'd been writing his alphabet. He grabbed his coat and slipped it on. His arms stuck out above his wrists. Paul's heart sank. Why hadn't he noticed? "Where do you think you're going, buddy?"

"To visit Bobbin. She can't get out and walk yet. Okay?"

"Me, too," Lester said, tossing a glare to Melissa.

Paul shot Bear a look before the boy could speak up and threaten to leave, too. There was no chance Paul would let himself be left alone with Melissa and risk being forced into a marriage he knew would bring him and the children nothing but trouble. He'd rather raise the children with his own inept two hands than to expose them to this young woman every day until they left home.

As a matter of fact, it was time he put the entire notion out of her head.

He gathered a deep breath as the younger boys escaped amid a blast of cold air. Paul had a feeling the subzero wind would be preferable to the chill that was about to invade this room.

❧

Try as she might, Grace couldn't keep Bobbin from pestering her. The little girl had gotten it into her head to finish a pair of mittens she'd begun knitting for Elmer last year. "I want to give them to him for Christmas."

Finally, Grace decided she had no choice and sat down with the girl at the table. "All right. Here's your problem: You missed three stitches up here. You'll have to unravel up to here." She showed the little girl where she meant. "Then start from there."

Grace scrutinized Bobbin's work. "You're actually doing quite a good job. Who taught you? Your ma?"

Bobbin's face saddened. "Yes, ma'am. . .miss."

"Well, you are a credit to her."

Bobbin's eyes softened. "You think so?"

"I certainly do."

A week had passed since the incident with Mr. Sands, and Grace was beginning to feel a little more confident that he had decided to let the matter pass. After all, what was there to do? His daughter was now a married woman—and glowing with the thrill of a new bride in love. The sergeant had found a tiny room behind the trading post where the two could set up housekeeping.

"Christmas is in only two more days. Do you think I'll have Elmer's mittens finished by then?"

"I don't see why not, if you work extra hard."

"I will, Miss Porter."

The door opened, and Melissa walked—no, floated—through the door. A smile curved her lips. She gave a sigh and moved to her bunk.

"What's wrong with you?" Bobbin asked.

"You wouldn't understand."

Grace couldn't resist a tiny smile. "Does this have anything to do with a certain lieutenant I noticed you speaking with yesterday?"

"He's asked to escort me to the Christmas dance tomorrow night."

"Did you say yes?"

Melissa jerked her chin, returning to her haughty self. "Not that it's any business of yours, but yes, I did. It will serve Paul right for the wretched way he treated me."

Although Melissa never came right out and admitted it, Grace surmised Paul had put an end to the girl's hopes of matrimony. She couldn't help but be a little bit happy that Melissa wasn't sulking. The girl was moving on, and with so many soldiers milling about the fort, Grace had the feeling Melissa wouldn't feel the sting of Paul's rejection for long.

Grace had decided to forego the dance and had somehow agreed to allow Elmer and Lester to keep Bobbin company while Paul ventured out for the first time since his feet had been frostbitten.

The next evening approached cold, to be sure, but with a beautiful starry sky. Grace stood just outside the door with Bobbin, watching the soldiers dressed in their best uniforms escorting lovely ladies dressed in silk, satin, and ribbons. But as beautiful as the people were, they were no match for the perfect night. *Was it in a sky like this one,* Grace wondered, *that the star appeared, leading the way to the birth of the Savior?* Her throat thickened at the thought.

Elmer and Lester arrived together. Paul followed. Grace's heart raced at the sight of him dressed in a fresh buckskin shirt. He must have traded with the Indians. His grin sent a wave of heat through her stomach. "I thought I'd better make sure they didn't get sidetracked on their way here."

"That was probably a good idea," Grace admitted. With the soldiers out and about and the festivities going on, the boys might have been tempted to get into mischief.

Paul hesitated. Grace held her breath, then slowly released it, as he captured her with his gaze. "I could stay here if you think you might need my help with the children."

Shaking her head, Grace averted her gaze. "We'll manage. As head of our wagon party, you need to be there. It's only proper."

"Then put on a pretty dress and come with me. I won't be able to dance much, but. . ."

"Yeah, Miss Porter," Lester said. "I'll look after the little ones."

Grace hated to disappoint Lester. He was just starting to come around again. At the very least, he could be persuaded to accept a cookie or two whenever he visited Bobbin.

"I'm afraid I have nothing appropriate to wear. Besides, the three of us have plans, remember?"

As one, the children nodded.

Paul frowned. "What plans? What are you four up to?"

Grace tried to hide it, but a smile broke through. "I expect you'll find out soon enough."

"All right. But all these secrets. . ."

"Don't even think about it," Grace said. In a moment of impulse, she gave him a playful little shove. "Off with you, now. Leave us to our plotting and planning."

Paul's face turned suddenly serious. He took her by her arms and looked into her eyes. So long, so seriously, Grace couldn't breathe. Even the stars seemed to stop glittering long enough to wait and see what he would do.

"Mr. Spencer?" Grace whispered. "What are you doing? The children are watching."

Her words seemed to pull him from whatever spell he'd been under. He released her. "Sorry," he muttered. "I best get going."

Clearing her throat, Grace pulled herself together. She

clapped as though announcing the end of lunch break as she'd always done during her school teaching days. "Well, children," she said, "shall we go inside?"

Lester kicked at the ground. Bobbin sighed. Elmer said, "Aw, rats."

"Whatever is wrong with you three?" she asked as they stepped inside.

"We thought Uncle Paul was going to ask you to marry him, that's all."

"How on earth would you come to that conclusion?"

Lester shrugged. "It was obvious."

"Well," Grace said, surprised to find herself amused by the embarrassing situation. "*Obviously* not, because he didn't, did he?"

"What would you say if he did?" Bobbin asked. The children had taken their seats around the table.

Grace looked from one hopeful set of eyes to the other. Her heart beat with compassion—no, it was more than that. Hers was a fondness that, in spite of her attempts to avoid any such thing, had risen dangerously close to maternal feelings of love. At least what she assumed were maternal feelings. She'd only felt this way about one other child, and that had ended in tragedy, because of her. "I would tell him thank you very much, but I have other obligations."

Hope turned to disappointment in each face.

"I told you so," Lester said with a sneer. "She don't want to be our ma."

"Lester, it's not that. . ." Grace began.

But Lester had risen to his feet and grabbed his coat. "I ain't stayin'."

"What about Uncle Paul's Christmas presents?" Elmer asked.

"You make them."

Before she could stop him, Lester ran out into the night.

sixteen

Grace stared at the closed door for only a minute, then made a quick decision. She turned to Bobbin. "Can you two stay here and work on your projects without me?"

Bobbin had completed Elmer's mittens earlier and was working on a scarf for Paul that was nearly finished. And Elmer was trying his hardest to carve a horse out of a block of wood. The two looked at her soberly. "We'll be okay, Miss Porter," Bobbin said. "I'll look after Elmer."

Grace touched Bobbin's face. "Thank you. I shouldn't be long. I just have to be sure he goes home."

Slipping her heavy wool shawl about her shoulders, Grace closed the door firmly behind her and headed toward Paul's cabin. "Les?" she called, knocking on the door.

Silence greeted her. Panic threatened. She beat harder. "Lester! If you're in there, you'd best open this door, or else!"

Without waiting another second, she grabbed the latch and threw the door open. Relief nearly weakened her knees as the boy sat on his bunk, his face illuminated by the glow of the firelight.

She sat next to him. "Why do you get so mad at me, Lester?"

"Why don't you like us?" he shot back.

"I do. Very much."

"You do not."

"It's impolite to call someone a liar—especially a woman."

"If you liked us, you'd want to be our ma."

"I like a lot of people. I can't be everyone's ma, can I?"

Lester didn't speak for a couple of minutes. Then he turned to her slowly. "I know Uncle Paul asked you. I heard him tell

Mrs. Clyde. You said no."

Sucking in a sharp breath, Grace knew there was no point in denying the truth. "You're right. But it's not because I don't care about you, Les. Please believe me, I'm not. . ." Grace stopped herself. What was she about to do? Unburden her heart at the expense of a twelve-year-old boy? "Just believe me. It's not about any of you children, nor is it because I don't care about your uncle. It's just the way things have to be. You're old enough to accept things like this without stomping off in such a temper. Don't you think?"

A shrug lifted the boy's shoulders. "I reckon."

"Shall we go back to my cabin, then? I'm sure Bobbin will need my help with the rest of your uncle's scarf. And I hate the thought of leaving a knife in Elmer's hands while I'm gone." A knot formed in Grace's gut at the very thought. How could she have been so stupid? What if the boy sliced off his finger? "Let's go, Les."

"You know I wasn't really mad at you."

Grace smiled as they walked outside, closing the door firmly behind them. "Could have fooled me."

"Maybe a little."

"It's all right."

"Is it?"

"Of course. There's nothing wrong with anger. It's an honest emotion." Grace tapped his shoulder. "The only time anger is wrong is when we allow our emotions to harm others. Then it becomes sin."

"I love you, Miss Porter. I expect you'd be just about the best ma in the world, next to my ma."

"Oh, Les, I wish you wouldn't say that." His raw emotions, so open and vulnerable, made it difficult for her not to rush into the dining hall where the dance was being held, grab Paul, and beg him to marry her this very second. There was nothing on earth she'd love as much as being these children's mother, or being Paul's wife. But even as she tried to conjure up a happy image of the six of them as a family, all she could see was Bobbin's face twisted in agony as the wagon wheel ran her over. And then Sammie. Always, Sammie's face haunted her.

Les moved ahead. As they approached her cabin, Grace quickened her steps, sensing danger. "Wait, Lester. Let me go first."

She opened the door slowly, relief flooding over her as she saw the two children still at the table where she'd left them moments earlier. "Look who came back with me." She walked inside, slipping out of her coat. Bobbin glanced up silently, her eyes filled with fear.

"Honey? What's wrong?"

She realized that the children weren't looking at her but over her shoulder. Turning slowly, Grace fought to control the swelling fear. She came face-to-face with Mr. Sands.

He staggered toward her, and the smell of liquor on his breath made her take two steps back.

"Mr. Sands," she asked, her voice shaking, hands trembling. "What are you doing here?"

"Where have you been, Martha?"

A boulder-sized knot formed in Grace's stomach. She fought her rising panic and forced her voice to remain calm. "Mr. Sands, look at me. I'm not Martha. I'm Grace."

Like a shot, he reached out, grabbing the back of her neck, and yanked her to him. Pain shot through her neck.

"Leave her alone!" Elmer yelled.

"No! Children." Grace fought the iron grip squeezing her, to no avail. Her eyes pleaded with the children. "Stay back."

"Where were you, Martha?" he asked again, his face close to hers. The whiskey on his breath nearly gagged her. "As if I didn't already know."

"P—please, Mr. Sands. I'm not Martha. Look at me. I'm Grace. Grace Porter. And these children belong to Paul

Spencer, the wagon master."

He shoved her to the bunk. "Don't tell me I don't know my own little girl."

Staggering to the table, he squatted down next to Bobbin. Reaching out, he fingered her braid. "I know my girl's red hair anywhere."

Grace slowly pulled herself up. She knew she couldn't make any sudden moves, but she had to cross the room to her own bunk and somehow pull her revolver out from under her pillow.

She prayed Bobbin wouldn't get feisty and say something to set him off.

"What do you have there, honey?" Mr. Sands asked.

"I'm making a Christmas present for my. . ." She drew a breath. "For my daddy."

Pleasure wiped across his face. "Is that so?"

"Yes, sir, but it's supposed to be a surprise."

"And I went and spoiled it, didn't I?"

Grace watched in awe as the little girl charmed the drunken man.

Lester caught her gaze. Grace nodded toward her bunk. He frowned. She nodded again and quickly put her hands together and pressed them to her ear. Hopefully, he would understand that she wanted him to lie down. She had a plan.

The gesture worked. He moved slowly. "You!" Mr. Sands stood. "Who are you?"

"Leonard," Grace interjected, picking up on Bobbin's cues, "the neighbors asked us to keep their boys tonight. Lester isn't feeling well. May I tuck him into bed?"

"I reckon. Hurry it up. I'm hungry."

"Yes, Leonard."

"Come, Lester," she said, walking toward the boy. "Let's get you into bed."

"Yes, Miss." He gasped. "Ma'am."

"It's all right," she whispered. "Lie down. I need to slip my hand under the pillow and get my gun."

He nodded.

"Hurry up, woman," Mr. Sands barked from across the room, slurring his words.

"Yes, Leonard." Grace slid her hand under the pillow and fingered the small barrel. She slipped the weapon from its hiding place and tucked it into the folds of her skirt, just under her apron.

She turned just as Mr. Sands turned his attention to Elmer. "And what are you making there?"

"Making a horse for my uncle Paul."

Leonard's expression clouded with confusion. "Oh yeah? Not your pa, like my girl here?"

"My pa's dead. So's my ma. And if you hurt Miss Porter again, I'll stab you with my knife."

"Elmer!" Grace moved faster than she'd ever thought possible. She stepped in front of him before Mr. Sands could stagger across the table. He reached for Elmer but caught Grace instead. His hand landed on her throat, choking.

True to his word, Elmer raised his knife. "Elmer, no!" Grace reached out in the nick of time and grabbed his wrist before he could land his mark on Mr. Sands. "Drop it." She fought to speak.

"No! I'm not going to let him hurt you."

Bobbin hopped up, barely able to stand. "Me, neither. I ain't your girl!" she yelled.

"What is this?" Mr. Sands spoke an inch from her face. "You've poisoned my Tilly's mind against me?"

Fighting to stay conscious as he continued to squeeze, Grace whispered, "She's not Tilly, Mr. Sands."

"I ain't Tilly," Bobbin screamed. "I ain't Tilly. I ain't Tilly!"

Mr. Sands turned and stared hard at Bobbin. Clarity

replaced a cloud of confusion. He released Grace's throat. "She's not Tilly."

"No." Grace rubbed her throat, fighting to return to full consciousness. "It's Bobbin."

"Paul Spencer's girl."

"Yes."

"Well, that's good enough. He took my girl away from me." Moving much faster than before, Mr. Sands snatched Bobbin from the chair, flung her over his shoulder, and headed for the door. "You tell Paul I said an eye for an eye."

Grace knew she had no choice. She brought out the gun from beneath her apron. "Mr. Sands, I will not allow you to take that child out of this house."

He stopped and turned. "Do you think you're going to shoot me?"

"I would hate to, but yes, I will."

"You might hit the child."

Grace knew he was right. It would take every bit of skill she'd learned from her father and all of her courage to actually squeeze the trigger, but she'd do it. "I might. But you're a much larger target. I'm sure I'd get you."

Silently, she prayed for wisdom and a clear shot if necessary. As soon as she prayed, the image flashed: Sammie's pa, weeping as they hauled him away to jail. "My boy! I love him. I didn't mean it. Please, God, forgive me! Forgive me."

"You love your Tilly, Mr. Sands." She nearly gagged on the words, knowing his brand of love was more about bullying and control. Still, she had to try. "That's why you don't want her to leave you."

"It's too late." His eyes filled with tears. "She left. And it's all Paul's fault. And yours."

"Then punish us. I know as much as you love Tilly that you couldn't harm that sweet child just to get revenge. She's innocent."

Grace held her breath as he hesitated. "Please, let her go."

Drunken tears streamed down Mr. Sands's face. "If you take me, I can't finish Uncle Paul's scarf," Bobbin said. "Tomorrow is Christmas."

"Mr. Sands." Grace held her breath. She stepped forward, indicating the weapon in her hand. But she spoke calmly, careful to keep all hint of a threat from her tone. "Let her go. I beg you."

Mr. Sands took a breath and slid Bobbin from his shoulder just as the door burst open. Grace shot forward and snatched Bobbin into her arms. She held the child tight. Paul stood, shaking and breathless, his gun leveled at Mr. Sands. "What's going on here?"

"He was going to take Bobbin," Elmer said. "I was going to stab him, but Miss Porter wouldn't let me."

"Well, that's just as well. What do you have to say for yourself, Sands?"

Shoulders slumped, Mr. Sands appeared to have aged ten years. He shook his head. "Nothing."

"Let's go."

Paul looked at Grace. "Will you be okay here with the children for a little while? I'll be back as soon as I take him in."

Nodding, Grace buried her face in Bobbin's hair. "I'm so glad you're safe, sweetheart."

For the first time, Grace noticed the tears on her own face. When had she started crying? She slid Bobbin onto her chair; then she scooped up Elmer. "You brave, silly boy." She hugged him tight as tears continued to flow down her cheeks. "What on earth were you thinking?"

"I protected you, didn't I?"

"You sure gave it your best shot." Grace laughed through her tears.

Turning, she found Lester curled up on the bunk. Alarm seized her. Had he been hurt? She walked across the room and knelt on the floor next to the bunk. "Lester? Are you all right?"

He looked up at her, revealing tears. "I couldn't move," he whispered. "I wanted to help you. But I couldn't move."

Tenderness flooded through her soul. Reaching out, she brushed a lock of hair from his freckled forehead. "Son, you did move. When I needed you to, you lay down in the bed so I could get the gun."

"But I didn't protect you."

"What would you have done if you had been able to move?"

He gathered a shaky breath and sat up, swiping a sleeve across his nose. "I would have. . ." He turned and stared at the table as though trying to imagine the scenario where he was able to gain the upper hand and save them all. Finally he gave a helpless shrug.

"You see? You couldn't have done anything."

Any more than I could have. Her eyes widened at the thought. Could it be that she deserved the same amount of grace that Lester deserved?

"You saved us, Miss Porter." Bobbin limped across the room, followed by Elmer. They dropped to the floor on either side of her. "All of us."

"Does that mean you love us?" Elmer asked.

"More than I could possibly express."

Paul returned just then. Grace looked up, caught his gaze, and gave him the answer to the question in his eyes.

"I've always wanted a Christmas wedding," she said, her gaze unwavering. She stood as he walked across the room.

He took her hands in his. Elmer stood and hugged her waist from one side, while Bobbin took up residence on her other side.

The look in Paul's eyes took her breath away. "Why have you fought this so hard? You made me suffer immeasurably."

"May I tell you my story?"

Paul pressed their clasped hands to his chest. "I want to know everything that led up to this moment."

"There was a little boy named Sammie who attended my school." Her voice shook, but she refused to look down. "His mother died when he was very young, and he was being raised by his father, who had a need for the bottle. Every so often, Sammie came to school with bruises and once with a broken arm, but he always insisted he'd gotten them from one accident or another. I suspected his father. I went so far as to speak with the sheriff, but he had no authority to confront the man unless Sammie would accuse his father. Even then, it was unlikely anything could be done.

"One day, Sammie didn't come to school. I had a sick feeling in my stomach all day, and after I dismissed the children, I went to his house to find him. No one answered the door. I started to leave, but something compelled me to go back. I walked into the room and found Sammie against the wall."

Grace's voice faltered. Tears glistened in Paul's eyes, and he squeezed her hands, encouraging her to continue.

"I touched his head, but he was already cold. I kept feeling like it was my fault. If only I had pressed for the sheriff to investigate. Maybe it would have scared his pa, and he'd have stopped harming Sammie if he knew he was being watched. Or I thought, maybe I should have spoken to the man myself. Adopted Sammie, even."

"Is this the reason you stopped teaching?"

Grace nodded.

"And why you pushed the children away after Bobbin's accident?"

"I know it sounds silly. But I couldn't forgive myself and felt that the children were better off without me."

At her last words, the children let up a harmony of protest, all speaking at once and clamoring for her attention until Grace finally pulled her hands from Paul's and, laughing, gathered the three into her arms. "I don't believe that any longer." She looked up into Paul's eyes.

"I knew the minute they knocked me down that these hooligans needed me as much as I needed them. I just got sidetracked by my own guilt for a little while."

"When did you know I needed you?" He squeezed her hands, his smile tender, teasing, but filled with love.

She smiled up at him, enjoying the warmth of his hands around hers. "About ten minutes later."

A chuckle rumbled his chest. "Me, too." He eyed the children. "You three move aside and give me a chance to get close to Miss Porter."

Without being told twice, they obeyed and stepped back.

Grace's heart fluttered as Paul slipped his arms about her waist and pulled her close. "A Christmas wedding, huh?"

"If you don't mind."

Amusement squinted his eyes. "I'd marry you this second."

Laughter bubbled to Grace's lips. "You'll have to wait until tomorrow."

Paul lowered his face. "You're worth it." His lips met hers in a soft, clinging kiss—her first.

Lester groaned. "I knew this would happen. Grown-ups always have to kiss."

Grace laughed and turned to her new son. His face glowed red, but a grin tipped his lips.

Paul hooked her chin and turned her face back to his. "Tomorrow?"

She nodded, and suddenly everything and everyone around them faded until it was as though there were no one else in the room.

"This means no Oregon City hotel," he said. "Are you willing to give that up?"

"Oh, Paul. I was running away from my guilt. That's the only reason I was going to be a housekeeper. But God knew that I was really running to you." She glanced around the room. Her eyes lit on Bear in the doorway. He grinned. "To all of you. I only want to be where you are."

Amid cheers from their children, Paul wrapped her in his arms. Grace knew that God had brought her to this place at the best time of the year: On the day when the world celebrated the birth of God's Son, Grace and Paul would always celebrate the day He had made them into a family.

epilogue

Oregon, 1872

"Mama, may I hang the wreath on the door?"

Grace smiled at Bobbin. During the past five years, she had grown from a precocious child into a lovely girl, soon to be making the slip into womanhood. But not too soon, Grace hoped. She couldn't be more pleased with this daughter of her heart than if Bobbin had been her own flesh and blood.

"Yes, hang it," she replied, setting another log in the fireplace. "Everyone should be arriving soon."

Paul had resisted building a separate fireplace in the dining room, but seeing how much it meant to Grace, had relented. Grace smiled at the memory of how many times he'd admitted the dining room wouldn't be nearly as cozy and inviting without that small addition.

Especially at Christmastime. They had become a family at Christmas, so the holiday held a special significance for them in addition to being the birth of their Savior. On this Christmas Eve, the house was filled with delicious aromas coming from the kitchen. Most of the treats wouldn't be enjoyed until the next day, but cookies and apple tarts would be put out tonight while they opened gifts.

All of the children, including Bear and his bride, Valerie, and their two-year-old twins, would be spending the night. The couple had remained in love, and when Bear turned seventeen, they'd finally been allowed to marry. Younger than Grace would have liked, but she had to admit their love and devotion to one another and their children certainly couldn't be denied.

Paul and Grace had added two children, a boy and a girl, to the family, and soon another would make his or her entrance into the world.

The door burst open, bringing with it a fresh rush of cold December air. Bear filled the doorway, his arms loaded down with gifts.

"Merry Christmas, Mama Grace," he said, his eyes shining. "Where do you want these?"

"Under the tree, of course."

He returned in a moment and dropped a kiss on her cheek. He'd grown a mustache since Thanksgiving.

"It tickles." She smiled and patted his cheek.

"Valerie isn't crazy about it, but she hasn't ordered me to shave yet."

"Where are they?"

"Still at home."

Grace frowned up at her stepson. "Nothing is wrong, I hope."

Bear shook his head. "The twins got into the flour. Val's getting them cleaned up and will drive over with Lester."

Grace smiled at the image of those two girls covered in the white powder. They were certainly their pa's girls.

Bear's face softened as he looked at Grace's bulging belly. "You're looking well."

Grace waved him away. "I've gained too much weight this time. Your pa can barely help me up from a chair anymore."

"Where is Uncle Paul?"

"I'm here."

Grace's heart thumped as her husband strode into the dining room and wrapped her in his arms from behind. Leaning against his chest, Grace relaxed, all the tension and busyness of the day slipping from her shoulders as she gave way to his strength.

This was the strongest lesson Grace had learned—to surrender, to allow Paul to help lift her burdens, to allow his love for her to heal the memories and pain of the past.

"Have you seen Elmer?" she asked.

"In the barn, reading."

"You didn't tell him to come inside?"

Paul slipped a kiss on her cheek. "He promised he'd be along soon."

Grace shook her head. "That boy. He loses all track of time when he's got a book." She turned in her husband's arms. "You got the turkey for tomorrow, I hope."

He grinned. "Yes, ma'am. The bird is in the kitchen, cleaned and ready for you to stuff and cook in the morning."

"I'd best go look to it then."

"Wait," Paul said, lacing her swollen fingers in his. "Come with me."

"Where? I have so much work to do."

Bear smiled. "We'll take over, Mama Grace."

Amid her protest, Paul led her into their bedroom. In the corner, their fourteen-month-old daughter, Sarah, slept peacefully, sucking on her fist. "What is it?" Grace whispered.

"You've worked too hard today. I want you to lie down for a while."

"What?" Grace stared at her husband. "Are you serious? Paul, I don't have time to lie in the bed. There's work to do."

"Not for you." He gently pressed her back onto the bed. Bending over, he hooked her chin, and raised her face to his. Grace surrendered to his kiss. "Now lie down," he whispered. "I want you off your feet for at least an hour. Try to sleep if you can."

Too tired to fight, Grace lay back.

Paul sat at the foot of the bed. He unhooked her boots and pulled them from her feet.

Grace sighed. "You spoil me," she murmured as her body gave up all tension.

"You deserve it. I love you forever, my Grace."

A smile lifted the corners of her lips. As she gave up the fight and drifted to sleep, Grace knew she didn't need to dream. Reality was so much better.

A Letter To Our Readers

Dear Reader:

In order that we might better contribute to your reading enjoyment, we would appreciate your taking a few minutes to respond to the following questions. We welcome your comments and read each form and letter we receive. When completed, please return to the following:

Fiction Editor
Heartsong Presents
PO Box 719
Uhrichsville, Ohio 44683

1. Did you enjoy reading *A Season for Grace* by Tracey Bateman?
   ❑ Very much! I would like to see more books by this author!
   ❑ Moderately. I would have enjoyed it more if

   _____

   _____

   _____

2. Are you a member of **Heartsong Presents**? ❑ Yes ❑ No
   If no, where did you purchase this book? _____

   _____

3. How would you rate, on a scale from 1 (poor) to 5 (superior), the cover design? _____

4. On a scale from 1 (poor) to 10 (superior), please rate the following elements.

____	Heroine	____	Plot
____	Hero	____	Inspirational theme
____	Setting	____	Secondary characters

5. These characters were special because? _____
_____
_____

6. How has this book inspired your life? _____
_____
_____

7. What settings would you like to see covered in future
   Heartsong Presents books? _____
_____
_____

8. What are some inspirational themes you would like to see
   treated in future books? _____
_____
_____

9. Would you be interested in reading other **Heartsong
   Presents** titles? ❑ Yes ❑ No

10. Please check your age range:
    ❑ Under 18   ❑ 18-24
    ❑ 25-34   ❑ 35-45
    ❑ 46-55   ❑ Over 55

Name _____
Occupation _____
Address _____
City, State, Zip _____

MISSOURI
Brides

3 stories in 1

Hope is renewed in three historical romances by Mildred Colvin. Missouri of the early 1800s is full of exciting growth, but for three women, it is filled with lost hopes.

Historical, paperback, 368 pages, 5³/₁₆" x 8"

Heartsong

Any 12
Heartsong
Presents titles
for only
$27.00*

HISTORICAL ROMANCE IS CHEAPER BY THE DOZEN!

Buy any assortment of twelve *Heartsong Presents* titles and save 25% off of the already discounted price of $2.97 each!

*plus $4.00 shipping and handling per order and sales tax where applicable. If outside the U.S. please call 740-922-7280 for shipping charges.

HEARTSONG PRESENTS TITLES AVAILABLE NOW:

(If ordering from this page, please remember to include it with the order form.)

Presents

Great Inspirational Romance at a Great Price!

Heartsong Presents books are inspirational romances in contemporary and historical settings, designed to give you an enjoyable, spirit-lifting reading experience. You can choose wonderfully written titles from some of today's best authors like Wanda E. Brunstetter, Mary Connealy, Susan Page Davis, Cathy Marie Hake, Joyce Livingston, and many others.

When ordering quantities less than twelve, above titles are $2.97 each.
Not all titles may be available at time of order.